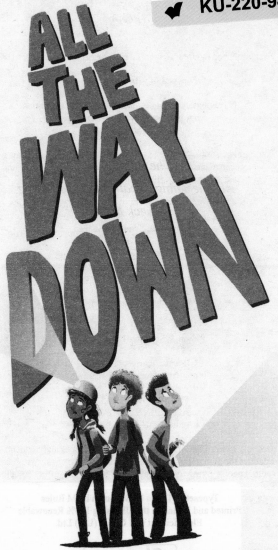

ALL THE WAY DOWN

STEWART FOSTER

SIMON & SCHUSTER

For Jon
(Beep)

First published in Great Britain in 2023 by Simon & Schuster UK Ltd

1 3 5 7 9 10 8 6 4 2

Simon & Schuster UK Ltd
1st Floor, 222 Gray's Inn Road
London WC1X 8HB

www.simonandschuster.co.uk
www.simonandschuster.com.au
www.simonandschuster.co.in

Simon & Schuster Australia, Sydney
Simon & Schuster India, New Delhi

A CIP catalogue record for this book
is available from the British Library.

PB ISBN 978-1-3985-1731-8
eBook ISBN 978-1-3985-1732-5
eAudio ISBN 978-1-3985-1733-2

SLEEPING WITH THE LIGHT ON

AWARDS FOR HEROES

'Is Effie here?'

'I'm not sure, love, but I can't see her.'

'But she's coming, yeah?'

Mum puts her hand on my shoulder as I scan the crowd gathered around the stage inside Wembley Arena. 'Milo,' she says, straightening my tie, 'I know you're anxious, but she'll be here. You'll see. Maybe go talk to Oscar.'

Oscar's standing in a corner with his mum and dad, surrounded by cameras and reporters. He's smiling like nothing happened, like all he did was get lost in a shopping centre.

I wish I could be like him.

I wish I had a smile that lights up in the dark.

I wish ... I wish ...

'Milo? Is it Milo?'

I jump. I'm always jumpy since *it* happened.

1

A reporter stands beside me. No camera, just a microphone in her outstretched hand.

'Were you scared? What was it like down there? Was there ever a time you thought you'd never get out?'

Yes, very scared. Horrible. All the time. I think all these things, but no words come out of my mouth, because all I can remember is the darkness and the tunnels, so narrow I could barely squeeze my body through.

Another reporter appears out of nowhere: 'Milo, how does it feel to be here, at the Awards for Heroes ceremony?'

'Can you just tell us what it was like in those final hours?'

I stare ahead, wishing I could avoid their questions, wishing I could get out of this suit or at least take the jacket off, but Mum's already told me ten times I can't because everyone else looks so smart.

Across the room, Oscar's stopped talking and is staring back at me.

The reporter is still asking questions: 'Milo? Those final hours?'

'I think maybe it's best that you talk to him later.' Mum steps forward. 'He's a little overwhelmed. You know, the stage, the cameras, the whole occasion . . .' Her words fade away.

Oscar's pulling at his tie, looking trapped in his suit too. He's still staring at me, and me at him, like we're sending silent invisible messages across the crowded room.

Effie?

Is she here?

Is she okay?

I don't know.

I walk towards Oscar, my stomach flipping with nerves.

2

I want him to say yes. I want him to know. Effie said she was coming, she messaged last night, she's messaged every night since it happened. Or maybe it was *me* messaging *her*, at seven, at eight, at nine in the evenings.

I can't stop myself.

Can't help myself.

I'm okay during the day, but not when it's dark.

We'll feel better if we're together like we were before – me, Effie and Oscar. It's like we carry a magic pill for each other that calms us down. But it doesn't work if one of us is missing.

We're like a shopping trolley with a jammed wheel, spinning in circles, smashing into cans of tomato soup, spilling them down the aisle. It's called the missing third wheel. That's what Diara, my counsellor, says. And it's only to be expected, after what –

Me and Oscar stop dead in our tracks. The heads of the crowd have turned towards a door by the stage.

The reporters rush forward. Suddenly there's more cameras, more noise, more flashing lights, and between the sea of bodies and heads ... Effie? Is that Effie? If it is, all I can see is her black hair, as she's got her head down, with two security guards in front of her, clearing a path like she's a movie star.

Leave her alone.

Leave her alone.

Me and Oscar pull at the bodies, at the arms holding the cameras.

It wasn't supposed to be like this. We thought it would just be a presentation in a room. A handshake and a certificate, like kids getting an award at school. This feels like the whole world is watching.

3

Me and Oscar keep pushing, keep pulling through the mass of people. Last arm. Last body.

'Effie,' I shout. 'Effie!'

The crowd parts and she's right in front of me. Dark hair, sparkling eyes ... but it's not her. It's Carly Wyatt from morning TV. Dom Fox, another presenter, is here too. Carly smiles at me, smiles at Oscar and shakes our hands. And Dom shakes our hands too, then says something like, 'Lovely to meet you.' I don't know exactly what because the cameras are whirring and the lights are flashing, blinding us, just like they did the day we came up. And the reporters are back at me and Oscar again.

'What's it like?'

'How proud are you to be awarded the Awards for Heroes medal?'

Phones and recording devices are shoved in front of us; there's a sharp pain behind my ear as an elbow knocks against my head.

Me and Oscar huddle together. We're back in the dark again.

Take deep breaths. Take deep breaths.

Do we feel better?

Yes, we feel better.

'Okay, please clear the way, please clear the way.'

Oscar's smiling. I'm squirming. We've lost our parents in the crowd but at least we're together.

'We're famous, Milo! Told you we'd be famous!' I hear Oscar's voice in my ear as we make our way to the side of the stage.

Oscar did say we would be famous, but then we all said a lot of things while we were down there – it feels like we talked for ever, so long we know all each other's hopes, dreams and fears. We said we'd keep them to ourselves and tell no one when we got out. But kids at school want to know what we talked about, our parents too, and now the reporters here at the arena. They want to know everything, but down in the dark, we made a pact – tell no one. No one. Agreed? Agreed.

Dom Fox and Carly Wyatt walk onto the stage and the audience applauds; I flash a look over my shoulder. Still no Effie. Where is she? Oscar only had to spend a couple of hours on the train from Brighton, and it took Mum and Dad just under three hours to get here from Bristol, but Effie said it would take her five hours from North Wales. She said she was coming the day before, and staying in a hotel like I was, but I didn't see her there.

I tap Oscar on the shoulder. 'Oscar,' I say. 'Effie! Where is she?'

'Who knows!' He smiles as a TV camera points at our faces. He's trying to be cool, but I know him: underneath he's as nervous as me. I look to my left, then my right, and suddenly realise there are other children here. Not just us. Some smiling, some talking, some holding their parents' hands tightly.

The applause dies away and the lights suddenly dim around us.

My chest cramps.

No, please put the lights on. Please turn them back on!

Panicking, I search for Oscar's hand, but he's already gripping mine and we pull each other close – take deep breaths, take deep breaths, try to smile for the cameras. Neither of us have spoken about it since it happened, to each other or Effie. Our messages have been jokes about what we've been doing, full of smiley emojis. It's like we were saving all our words up until we got here, but now we're struck dumb.

5

'Good evening, everyone,' says Carly. 'Welcome to the Awards for Heroes. Dom and I are so happy to be here.'

Dom Fox steps forward. 'Yes,' he says. 'As always, we have so many heroes, so many amazing tales, so much bravery, from children who have overcome mental and physical disability, to children who rescued their parents from a fire. And they are all here with us tonight.'

The crowd stands up and applauds. I spot my mum and dad in the crowd, clapping, but from the looks on their faces I know they're wondering whether I'm okay. I don't want them to think I'm angsty, not when they've made such an effort to be here. Mum took a day off from her dog-grooming business and Dad only knew he could make it at the last minute, because he's a paramedic and might have had to work if a colleague didn't turn up. I try to smile, to convince them I'm okay, as slowly the applause dies down.

'So,' says Dom Fox, 'these guys are going to take their seats while we begin with our first story, our first hero. Six-year-old Leah, from Milton Keynes . . .'

I follow Oscar off the stage as a picture of a mousey-haired girl fills the screen. And then I see her in real life by the steps, standing with her parents. She has bandages wrapped around her hands. Suddenly I feel like I shouldn't be here. These children are real heroes, they've saved people.

What did we do?

Get stuck in a mine with no way out.

And one of us isn't here. One of us is missing. As me and Oscar take our seats in the front row, I notice his smile has dropped, and he looks like he's about to cry.

'Oscar,' I whisper. 'You okay?'

'The dark,' he says, gripping the arm of his seat. 'I hate it.'

'Me too,' I say. 'Ever since it happened, I . . .'

Oscar looks around like he's worried someone is listening, but everyone else is watching Dom Fox as he talks to Leah and her parents.

'You what, Oscar?' I say.

'You won't laugh,' says Oscar.

'No, I won't laugh.'

'It feels stupid,' he says. 'I'm eleven . . . Maybe I'll just ask. Yeah, I'll just ask.'

'Ask what, Oscar?'

'Do you sleep with the light on?'

I sigh with relief. I've been keeping quiet about that for weeks. 'Yeah,' I say. 'I haven't turned my bedroom light off since I got home. Some nights I'm too scared to close my eyes.'

'Every night,' says Oscar.

'Yeah, every night, and when I do get to sleep, I –'

I pause as a picture of the three of us flashes up on the screen.

Dom Fox walks back onto the stage.

'That was a lovely story, and we'll be hearing more from Leah later,' he says. 'But now, for the next half an hour or so, we're going to relive the story that captivated us all during the summer – the mine collapse in Cornwall.'

Oscar leans close to me. 'Tell me a chicken joke, Milo,' he whispers.

'What, here?'

'Yeah,' he says. 'Make us feel less nervous.'

I chuckle, and try to think of a chicken joke, but I've not told one

7

since we came up. 'I'll do it later,' I say. The audience is applauding as the words 'heroes' flashes under our pictures on the screen.

We both sit back and watch. I wish I could tell him a chicken joke, to make us both laugh. I need to laugh. I need something to help me forget, because every night, when I go to sleep, I'm trapped inside a nightmare, scraping away the dirt in the dark and he and Effie have gone.

Everyone is gone.

And I want them back.

I want everyone back.

But one of us is missing, and I'm looking around the hall, because I need Effie. I need her right now.

CHAPTER 1

EIGHT WEEKS BEFORE

WHO? WHERE? *WHY?*

It was 16th August, the first day at camp in Cornwall. Twelve of us were standing in a circle, nervously trying to work each other out: who's the cool one, who's the nerd, who might be my friend, who's the one we'll all hate and avoid for the next seven days? I'd scanned them all and now I stood with my head down, staring at the dust that shone like slivers of silver in the early-morning sun.

It was like we were contestants on a game show.

And the first prize is a month-long trip to Disneyland!
Ha, if only.
But if it was, you'd take me, Milo?
Of course, Lukey. I'll take you everywhere with me. I
brought you here, didn't I?
Yep. Thanks ☺

That was my six-year-old brother, Luke, chatting away in my head. And you might think that strange, but why wouldn't you imagine taking the person you love most with you everywhere even though he is –

Why did the chicken wear sun cream?
Not now, Lukey. I'm trying to listen.
Go on, Milo. Just one. Why did the chicken wear sun cream?
I don't know, why did the chicken wear sun cream?
Because it didn't want to get roasted ... Is that a good one?
Yeah. I smiled to myself. That's a good—

'Milo.' Dad tapped me on my shoulder. 'You need to listen to the instructors.'

'It's okay,' I said. 'I am.' And I was, it's just that I was listening to Luke too.

There were four instructors, and they'd just introduced themselves – Trey, Sabula, Lois and Matty. Trey looked about the same age as Dad, but with triple the number of muscles bulging out of his T-shirt, and the others were maybe ten years younger. They were all wearing red T-shirts, sunglasses and yellow caps with a bird logo on the peak. They were there to help us, they said. Help us have a good time and enjoy ourselves. And they were standing in front of a banner that read: WELCOME TO SWALLOW HEIGHTS.

Trey stepped forward, taking off his sunglasses. 'So, you've heard

10

a little about us,' he said. 'Who we are and what we do. So how about we all hear a little bit about you?'

Some of the group smiled. Nervous smiles, or at any rate mine was. Some of the others shrugged, like they were thinking, *What do we do now?*

'Come on,' said Sabula, taking her hat off and retying a hairband, then putting the hat back on. 'You've all come a long way and you're going to be here a week. So just start with names.' She spoke in a Birmingham accent that sounded just like my Auntie Marie.

I shuffled my feet in the dust.

> *Aren't you going to speak?*
> Not yet.

'Just your names,' said Trey, 'Nothing more, just that and maybe where you come from. Oh, and in case you're wondering, yes, you do all get to wear these cool outfits.'

'Lucky you,' said Matty.

It was like they were trying to get us all to relax, but if the others in the group were anything like me, their nerves must have been growing with every kilometre we travelled to this place, leaving our homes far behind. We knew nothing about each other, where we were from, or why we were here, only that we were all in Year Seven at our schools.

So, nobody spoke. The only sound was the wind whistling across the dust.

A woman who was dressed too smartly to be here nudged a boy with spiked black hair in the back.

'Go on, Os—'

'No!' the boy shouted before the woman could finish saying his name. 'I don't want to. What am I doing here anyway?'

'But –'

'I said no! Leave me alone!'

'It's okay,' said Trey. 'No one's forcing you.'

'Except her,' said the boy. 'You're so embarrassing, Mum.' I noticed his brand-new Nike trainers, and what looked like the latest iPhone in his hand.

The woman stepped back and held up her hands as if to say, 'Well, I tried.'

I glanced back at my dad. He nodded ahead, like I should be paying attention to the instructors.

More looks. More silence. I hated the silence, but I didn't want to be the one who broke it because everyone would look at me. If Luke was actually here, he'd say something funny that would get everyone laughing.

Why did the chicken –
Not now, Lukey.
Okay, then speak. Introduce yourself. Come on, Milo.
I said I didn't want to.
Okay, then I'll go. Hi, my name is Lu—
Okay.

'Okay!'

Bit loud.

12

I looked up. Everyone was staring at me, like I'd done something wrong.

'Milo,' I said, clearing my throat. 'My name is Milo ... and we're from ... I mean, *I'm* from Bristol.'

'Pleased to meet you, Milo from Bristol,' said Sabula.

I sighed, relieved.

> *Because you were glad you went first?*
> Because they didn't notice I nearly mentioned you.
> *Oops.*

Dad tapped me gently on the shoulder, then I felt the warmth of his breath on my ear. 'Good lad, Milo,' he whispered. 'Well done.'

> *Yes, well done, Milo.*
> Thanks.

'Who's next?' asked Lois. She was the smallest of the instructors, so small she could have been one of us kids. 'Anyone?'

One by one every member of the group said their name and where they came from, but none of them stuck in my mind. Not because of Luke, but because I was too busy looking at the grey buildings that stood in the dust behind them. All the same size, with the same low roofs, the same dark hollowed-out windows. They looked like they used to house soldiers. The only difference was the signs that hung above the doors – SHOWER BLOCK AND TOILETS, DORMS, MEETING ROOM and STAFF. And behind the buildings, up in the distance, was the mine, a tower of rusty crisscrossed metal casting a shadow down from the hill.

> *Like Iron Man found an old satellite in space and*
> *planted it on Earth.*
> Good one.
> *You can put it in one of the stories you write, if you like.*
> Thanks, I'll do it later.
> *Okay.*

'Right.' Matty clapped his hands, like he was trying to wake us all up. 'Well done, now all that's left is for you to say your goodbyes to the people who brought you.'

The boy who had shouted stood next to me, arms folded, staring straight ahead. He said he didn't want to be here, but he was ignoring the person who could take him home. People say I'm quiet now and shut myself away, but I love my dad so much that I could never let him go without saying goodbye.

> *Me neither.*

I turned round slowly. Dad was knelt down, his face close to mine.

> *Hi, Dad* 😊

'You'll be okay, Milo,' he said. 'Just think of this time as something that could help. We'll be together again soon. It's only for a week,

14

after all.' He stood up. 'And how about I take this?' he said, tugging at my parka. 'I really don't think you're going to need it in this weather. Everyone else is wearing hoodies or T-shirts.'

I looked down at my coat. The bottom only came down to my waist and the sleeves ended halfway between my wrists and my elbows. I was hot, and even I knew I looked silly in it, but it was Luke's and there was no way I'd let Dad or anyone else take it away from me.

And I think Dad knew because he didn't ask again. He just smiled at the instructors, then reached into his pocket for his car keys.

> *Don't let him go.*
> He has to.
> *But I don't want him to. I don't want him to leave us here, Milo. Don't –*

'Don't leave us,' I blurted.

Luke, you've got to stop making me do that.

'What's that?' Dad asked. 'I couldn't hear because of the wind.'
   'Nothing,' I said.

Nothing?

'You sure?'
   Zip lips!

15

Dad put his finger gently on my forehead and brushed my fringe out of my eyes. 'Sometimes I wonder what you're thinking under there.'

He doesn't know.
And we can't tell him.

'I'm okay, Dad,' I said.

Dad looked at me for a long time.

'Love you, Milo.'

'Love you too, Dad,' I said.

'Yeah.' He smiled, then ruffled my hair. 'I know you do.'

He wrapped his arms around me, and I felt him shaking like he couldn't hug me enough.

I wish I could hug him back.

I wished I could hug him too, like everyone else, except the boy who had shouted, was doing to their parents. But I stood stock still, hands down at my sides. I could have said, 'I love you,' but sometimes I think I'm so numb that Dad must feel like he's hugging a stone. What he didn't know was that I didn't think it was fair on Luke, to hug him when he couldn't. But nothing was fair since Luke had gone. It wasn't fair that Mum told herself off whenever she called me Luke by mistake, and it wasn't fair that I felt bad when she did. And if wasn't fair that Dad had to drive an ambulance every day, to the same hospital where Luke had stayed. He said it was okay, that it was his job, but as Dad walked towards the parked cars with the rest of the parents, I wanted to run after him, tell him not to leave me, tell him he didn't have to go to work, but my feet were stuck to the ground. All I could do was force a smile and wave as the cars all pulled away, with dust pluming from their wheels.

And then I was alone. Not *alone* alone, because of course I still had Luke. And even though I wanted to go with Dad, I knew I had to stay. Mum and Dad said I needed help. I knew I did, but did it have to be with a group of strangers, in a dustbowl three hundred kilometres from home?

'Right,' said Matty, clapping his hands. 'Now they've gone, let's get you lot digging holes.'

'What?' asked a girl with red hair.

'I'm joking,' said Matty.

'Ha, great joke,' said the boy who'd shouted.

'Thought you'd appreciate that, Oscar,' said Matty. 'So no, we're not here to dig holes, but we are here to have fun. So, grab your rucksacks. Girls, follow Sabula and Lois and they'll show you your dorm. Boys, me and Trey will show you yours.'

Oscar scuffed his feet through the dust and picked up a blue rucksack. And as the rest of the group picked up theirs, I knew I should get mine too, but I was still stuck to the spot, watching the dust settle on the hill.

A week is a long time.
I know.
Seven days ... And what did Trey mean about
digging holes?

17

It was a joke, about a book called *Holes*.
Have we read it?
Yes. Well, I have. It was a bit old for you. But I could
read it again.

'You coming, Milo?' Trey shouted. 'You'll miss picking a bed.'

We'd better go.
Yeah.

As usual, I was the last in line, the last to be ready. Since Luke had gone,
it had been that way – *Milo, are you waiting for a bus? Milo, you'd forget
your head if you could. Milo, are you part of this class?* But there wasn't
a bus, and I never forgot my head, and I was part of the class. It was just
that I always took Luke to school with me, and I liked it that way.

As the others went inside, I took a last look around.

Why are we here, Lukey? Why are we here?

Luke didn't answer. It was like he'd worked out why before I had.

A swirl of dust travelled across the ground.

So dusty, Lukey, So dusty.

So dusty it was like we'd been left on the Moon, without a spaceship
to get us back home.

CHAPTER 2

DODGEBALL / *WE LOVE THE LION*

'Not too bad, is it?' Oscar bounced up and down on the bed next to mine. 'The mattresses, I mean. A bit spongy, and the pillows are as hard as rocks, but it's okay.'

Friend or enemy?

I smiled as I remembered me and Luke playing friend or enemy on the way home from school. It was like me teaching him about stranger danger, except deciding whether someone was our friend or our enemy was more fun.

So, which is he?
Don't know. Too early to tell.

'Try yours.' Oscar continued bouncing.

I put my bag gently down on my bed, still trying to work Oscar out.

'What?' He grinned. 'Wondering why I'm suddenly happy?'

I shrugged.

'It was an act, earlier,' he said, nodding out of the window at the

19

instructors standing in the dust. 'You've got to make them think you're not enjoying it, or not getting better. That way you get to come again. I mean, this place is in the middle of nowhere, but that lot seem all right. That Matty looks a bit of a wimp, but the Trey bloke looks like he could rip up trees.'

I smiled to myself as he picked up his rucksack and started to unpack. His clothes were neatly folded and he had a spare pair of Nikes that looked brand new. He kept talking all the time. He seemed to know loads about what was going to happen. All I knew was what Mum had found on the internet. 'It's like a school trip,' she'd said, one evening after tea. 'There's loads to do – rock climbing and kayaking.'

'It's even got a zip-wire,' Dad said, turning the laptop screen to face me. 'The longest and highest in Europe. You know, that makes me wish I was going myself!'

'It looks amazing,' said Mum. *Amazing. Amazing.* Her words repeated over and over in my head.

If it was so amazing, why did she cry when I left home that morning? But then everyone seemed to be crying since the last time we'd sat around Luke's bed, watching his heart *beep, beep, beep* on a machine – every night when I went to see him after school, all day when I went to see him at weekends. *Beep, beep, hiss, clunk. Beep, beep, hiss clunk.* Monitors to check his heart, machines to help him breathe. I'd talk to him all the time and read our book, like doing that might wake him up. But still the sound went on – *beep, beep, hiss, clunk. Beep, beep, hiss, clunk* – it followed me home to my bed, and to school the next day. *Beep, beep, hiss, clunk. Beep, beep, hiss, clunk* –

'Oi, hello.' Oscar waved his hand in front of my face. 'Anyone home?'

Bit rude.

I backed away.

'What?' I asked.

'I said, is this your first time?'

'Yes,' I mumbled. 'It's our ... my first time. I didn't know you could come twice.'

'Oh, only if you don't get better.' Oscar grinned, then leaned forward. 'Don't tell anyone, but it's way better than school. I've even been to places where they have swimming pools and waterslides. Anyway, Milo, what's your problem?'

'My problem?'

Your problem?

'Yeah.' Oscar looked up from his bag at the other three boys who were talking by their beds. 'We've all got problems,' he said, quietly. 'That's why we're here. I got anger issues, like you can't tell from when I kicked off at my mum. Sometimes I feel bad about that. It always comes out worse than I expected. Can't stop it. Maybe it isn't an act. Ah, yes! She did pack it!' He held up a black tin with writing on the side. 'Hair gel,' he said.

I smiled as his skin was so pale that his spiked hair made him look like he'd seen a ghost.

21

'Anyway.' Oscar put the tub on the table between our beds. 'What's your problem? Apart from wearing that weird coat.'

I shrugged.

'Nothing, really,' I said.

Nothing, really?

'Must be something,' said Oscar. 'OCD, ADHD, any other group of letters ending in D.' He spoke quickly, hardly leaving himself time to breathe.

'Nope,' I said. 'Nothing with a *D*.' Even though it was because of the worst *D* of all.

Oscar laughed. 'Don't say much, do you?'

Nope.

'Not really.'

'Oh well,' said Oscar, standing up. 'Guess we'll all find out soon enough, although sometimes they put us in with "normal" kids and it's hard to tell.' He walked towards the three boys on the other side of the room. Within a few seconds they burst out laughing, like Oscar had told them the funniest joke in the world. I wondered if it was about me or my coat. I was used to kids doing that at school. But I wasn't at school any more. I was at camp, making a new start, according to Mum.

I opened my rucksack, beside me on the bed. Mum had packed everything the week before, but every night after that she sat with me and went through the checklist like I would forget – toothpaste, toothbrush, six pairs of socks and pants, two pairs of shorts, a pair of jeans, a Bristol Rovers football kit and a Captain America T-shirt, and another with Iron Man on the front. I took them all out and put them in the locker by the side of my bed.

I unpacked the rest of my things until I reached my book –

> *Our favourite book!*
> Yep. *The Boy, the Girl . . .*
> *. . . and the Lion! I love the lion.*
> I know.
> *Can we read it now?*
> Later.

I put the book in the bottom drawer, then looked at my diary. Dad got it for me last Christmas. He told me that when he was my age he used to write his thoughts down, and maybe I'd like to do the same. I hadn't written a single word in it. But I still took the diary everywhere: to school, to town, to my friends' whenever I had a sleepover, because my diary wasn't to collect my thoughts, it was to store a picture. Right there in the middle between 25 and 26 June. As I found it again, I couldn't stop myself smiling as me and Luke were frozen, eyes wild, mouths open, our hair bleached blonder by the sun, as we screamed our way down what felt like the world's longest waterslide.

> *Aww, that's nice* ☺

It was.

'Come on, Milo.'

I snapped my diary shut. Oscar was right in front of me.

'We're all going outside to play dodgeball before tea.'

I put my diary under my pillow and walked outside. Trey was standing in the dust, handing out red T-shirts, hoodies and sunglasses. Oscar must have raced to the head of the queue because he'd already put his on and was running around, grabbing hold of anyone he could, asking, 'Do I look, cool? Do I look cool?'

Friend or enemy? Friend or enemy?

I still didn't know, but I did kind of find him funny.

'There's always one.' A dark-skinned girl with braids in her hair came and stood beside me. 'Or maybe I'm jealous because mine keep falling off.' She nodded her head, which made her sunglasses slip to the end of her nose.

I laughed, nervously.

'I'm Effie,' she said, holding out her hand like she guessed. 'That's Effie, not F. E . . . I said that when we were introducing ourselves,' she said. 'But you didn't seem to be paying much attention.'

That's because you were talking to me.
As usual.

'Yes,' I said. 'We were . . . I mean, I was a bit nervous.'

'Think we all are a bit,' she said. 'Except him, maybe.' She nodded at Oscar, who was now running around with his cap on backwards. 'But then we're all different, that's what my nan says. Well, actually she says life would be boring if we were all the same. You're from Bristol?'

'Yeah,' I said, wondering how she knew.

'You said . . . when you told us your name.'

'Oh right,' I said. 'Sorry.'

'I'm from Liverpool, like you can't tell from my accent, but I live with my nan in North Wales.'

Friend or enemy?
Stop with the friend or enemy, already.
Just saying.

'You'd better move,' said Effie.

'What?'

She pushed me. 'Move,' she said. 'Or you're going to be the first one out.'

A boy ran towards me. I jumped as he threw the ball and it bounced underneath me.

Ha! Missed!

I ran across the dust, towards the others, who were circling the boy with the ball, daring him to throw it.

He threw the ball again and hit a girl on the knee. The group shouted and cheered as she ran after it. It was like everyone had

25

become friends after ten minutes, smiling and cheering, like they had no problems at all. It made me think that maybe Oscar had got it wrong, that maybe we didn't all have a 'problem', but for weeks I'd overheard Mum and Dad whispering in the house.

'He'll get over it. Give him time.'

'It's hard for us all, but especially for him.'

'But he can't go on like this. We have to do something to help.'

At first, they'd said it was good that we talk about Luke, it was the best way to help us all cope. They'd say things like, 'If Luke was here, he would love this' and, 'I wonder what Luke would do now.' But I didn't have to wonder, I could just ask him, because from the start he was right there in my head.

I never told Mum and Dad, but I think they may have guessed. I used to hide in my room, with our picture on the waterslide. Luke had been taken away once; I didn't want him taken away again. It was bad enough that there was no one to race me up the stairs any more. No one to kick the football back or play swordfights with bananas.

'Milo, you're on it.'

Ooh, it's our turn.

The group were all around me. I didn't remember the ball hitting me, only seeing it bounce away.

'Milo! You're it,' Effie said again.

But I couldn't play. I just wanted to talk to Luke.

26

But if I was quiet, you could play. I could try it if you
want. Like I do when you're at school.
No, don't go quiet. I talk to you because I want to.

Luke?

Luke?

I hated the silence. I hated the gaps Luke left when he was gone. One
time in History class, he went missing so I could learn about the cause
of the First World War. And he was still missing in the lesson after.
But it didn't help me learn. I just spent the whole time searching for
him in my head, for so long that Mr Walker, my science teacher, told
me I was miles away, so many it was like I was on another planet.
But I was on Earth all the time, just wishing Luke was on it with me.

Okay, I'll come back, then! 😊
Thanks.

CHAPTER 3

FILM NIGHT / *NO SPIDEY* 🙁

I had butterflies in my stomach, still wondering why we were all here at camp as we ate tea that evening, wearing our red hoodies. I sat with Oscar and Effie and Kaya, another girl I'd got to know during dodgeball. As we scooped beans into our mouths, Trey told us about the things we would be doing during the week. Some were on the website Mum and Dad had shared with me ... but since then, more activities like Paddle-boarding, Go-karting and Archery had been added.

'That's the advantage of being in this dustbowl,' Matty said. 'We can do anything at all, and at any time, come rain, hail or sun. And of course, it wouldn't be right to bring you all this way without giving you a tour of the mine.'

'Yeah,' Oscar mumbled to me. 'But they missed out the bits where they try to get into our heads.'

'What's that?' asked Trey.

'Nothing,' said Oscar. 'Just said the beds were nice.'

'Hmm.' Matty gave Oscar a wary look. 'I'm not sure that's what you said, Oscar, but believe me, even *you* will have some fun.'

28

'As if.' Now Oscar shoved more beans into his mouth, then shrugged as he realised I was looking at him. 'What?' He grinned. 'I told you, you can't show you're enjoying yourself too much, or you don't get to come again.'

'I'm not sure how that works,' said Effie.

'Me neither.' Oscar shrugged. 'But I still do it.'

'Anyway,' Matty continued, 'when you've all stopped talking, who's up for a film?'

Me! Me!

Luke jumped into my head. I took a deep breath, hoping he would shush.

But I love films.
I know.

'What have you got lined up for us tonight, Sabula?'

Spider-Man! Spider-Man!

'We've got a choice,' said Sabula.

Spider-Man! Please, Spider-Man.

'Iron Man or Avengers.'

What? No! Spider-Man, Spider-Man. Tell them, Milo.
Why no Spider-Man? Why . . .

'No, Spider-Man!' I said.

Everyone turned and looked at me. I hadn't shouted that loud, but it was like they were already used to me being the quiet one.

You can't keep doing that to me, Lukey.
Sorry . . . again.

'Spider-Man wasn't one of the options,' said Sabula. 'But perhaps tomorrow night?'

'It's okay,' I said, desperately trying to cover my tracks. 'I meant Iron Man, anyway.'

'Weird,' mumbled Oscar. 'They don't even sound alike.'

Sabula smiled. 'It's okay, Milo,' she said. 'At least we know what you want. Anyone else for Iron Man?'

Six hands shot up for Iron Man.

I sat back in my chair, hoping no one had noticed my panic. Oscar shot me a weird look, like he had before, but Effie gave me a warm smile, then she leaned across the table and whispered, 'It's okay, Milo. I get my superheroes mixed up too.'

I smiled.

Friend or enemy?
Is she friend or enemy?
Friend . . . I think.

You think? She said a nice thing . . . and she smiled.
I know, but lots of people say nice things and smile.
Like when Mum used to get people to come
round after school, or you got invited out, after
I'd . . . you know.

I looked back at the screen and remembered how Mum used to take me to her friends' houses with her, to 'meet' their children, or make up weird reasons why I should have friends from school around mine – *Invite Zoe round to help with your maths homework. Ask Zac* (my best friend) *over, to play football in the garden.* And sometimes random friends would just turn up without her even telling me and we'd just sit drinking Coke and eating snacks. And we'd sip and crunch and they'd just look at me like they couldn't think of anything to say in between. But we knew what had happened, the *D*-word, and no one wanted to say it, especially not me. Because the *D*-word meant the end, and I didn't want that to happen. Not ever.

Iron Man was being attacked by Vanko and his electrified whips when my eyelids started to droop. Me and Dad had left home at seven in the morning, but I wasn't tired because I'd been up so long, I was tired because it was exhausting having Luke in my head all the time. Even worse, he kicked every kick, and dodged every bullet all the way through the film. He made me twitch so much that I had to pretend it was because I wanted to go to the toilet.

It's funny.

31

It's not.

Well, it is . . . just a bit.

Okay, just a bit.

When Iron Man had finally won his last battle, the group were allowed to sit and talk for an hour, before the boys and girls had to go to their separate dorms. At first it felt weird, like the instructors were listening in on us, as they sat in the corner of the room, by the fire, talking and looking at their phones. But soon everyone seemed to forget they were there. Oscar told us a ghost story about when he went on a school trip and stayed for a weekend in a church, and Ethan told us the reason his arm was in a cast was that he'd fallen off his scooter and broken it. Then we signed our names on the cast with a felt-tip pen. But we all stopped talking when Trey came over.

'Here we go,' whispered Oscar. 'Here comes the serious bit where they try to get into our heads. Just you wait.'

'Guys,' Trey said as he pulled up a chair. 'We've just been talking about the plan for tomorrow. It's going to be hotter than today, so we'll make an early start, get you down to the beach in the kayaks, have lunch, then depending on the heat, we'll either do the zip-wire or go down the mine. It's a lot cooler down there. Okay? Oh, and just to say, if any of you need anything, need to chat, come and find one of us. Yes, this week is all about adventure and having fun, but we all recognise that it might not be easy for some of you, being away from home. And we can talk about anything.'

Oscar nudged me. 'There you go,' he whispered. 'What did I tell you?'

Trey looked at him. I thought he was going to tell him off, but he just nodded at Oscar, like he was noting who the troublemaker was.

'As I was saying,' he turned to the rest of the group, 'come talk, about anything, any time. Oh, and before I forget, phones.'

'Phones?' asked Oscar.

'Yeah, phones,' said Trey. 'You know, the little pieces of plastic we all spend the whole of our lives on, texting and watching YouTube. We need to collect them before lights out.'

We all looked at each other like Trey had just told us the world was ending.

'Don't worry,' he said. 'You will get them back. We'll keep them in a safe place, and you can use them to contact your parents or guardians halfway through the week.'

'Like, Wednesday?' said Oscar. 'We can't have our phones till Wednesday! That's not fair. How am I going to contact all my friends?'

'Aw, Oscar,' said Trey. 'I'm sure they can cope without you for a few days.' He glanced at his watch. 'Anyway,' he said, suddenly standing up, 'five more minutes, then get ready for bed. Leave your phones in the plastic tray by the door.' He walked back to the others. Most of my group started talking, but all the time I could sense Oscar looking at me.

'What did I tell you?' he said. 'They say they want to talk, then take our phones away. This is like a prison camp.'

'Yeah,' said a boy wearing glasses – Malik, I think his name was. 'How are we supposed to order pizza?'

Some of the group laughed as we split up and went to our rooms.

Oscar got his phone out of his pocket. I thought how shiny and bright it looked compared to mine.

He glanced at me.

'It's just a phone,' he said. 'Dad gave it to me for my birthday, like that counts for anything.'

I thought of asking him what he meant, but he already had his head down, texting. 'Just telling all my friends,' he said. 'Tyler has an older brother, and I reckon I could get them to come down from Brighton and pick me up in his car then go back and drive along the seafront. Well, it's not actually his car, he kind of just borrows them off other people ... only he might not tell them.' He laughed.

Oscar's life seemed to be so exciting compared to mine: driving cars along the seafront, when most of the time I was sat in my room, chatting to Luke or writing stories.

I took my phone out of the drawer, hiding the cracked screen from Oscar. I checked my messages. One from Mum – *Missing you already, Milo, but you make sure you have a good time xxx*. Then there was one from Dad – *Only four hours to get back, am at work now. The instructors seem nice. The zip-wire looked* 😎. *Big love.*

I thought of messaging back, but Mum had been so upset when I left that I thought hearing from me might make her cry again. Oscar didn't seem to have any such worries because all the time I was overthinking, he was tapping furiously on his phone.

He stopped and looked up at me. 'You're so quiet,' he said.

'Am I?'

'Yeah, but that's okay. It means I can tell you anything and you won't tell anyone else.'

Except me. You tell me everything. And we don't need
text to chat . . . It must be our chat time soon.
Yeah, soon, Lukey.

I turned and started walking towards the door.

'See,' said Oscar, catching me up. 'You didn't even say anything
when I told you Tyler's brother is going to come and bust us out.' He
looked at his phone. 'Just waiting for a reply,' he said. 'But, hey, you
can come with us if you like. They're good fun. Last weekend he let
us have a go on the Downs where they race horses, then we drove back
to the seafront and we went on the dodgems on the pier.'

Yes, can we go?
No.
But we love dodgems! Remember when you bashed
into me and Dad and it knocked the hotdog out
of my hand?
Yeah.

I stopped walking.

'So, that's it,' said Oscar like he thought I was smiling in reply to
him. 'You're coming, then.'

Yes!
I don't think so.
Spoilsport.

'Tyler's not replied, but I sent a pin-drop on the map showing where ...' He stopped talking.

Trey was outside the door with the basket full of phones.

'Ah,' he said. 'I was just about to come looking for you two. I thought maybe you'd made a run for it, Oscar.'

He is! Tyler's brother is going to bust him out.

'Huh,' said Oscar as he dropped his phone into the basket. 'Who knows, I might.'

I didn't know whether to believe Oscar as the moon shone through the window over my bed that night. If you were going to get busted out, wouldn't you get your bags ready and go to sleep with your clothes on and not in your pyjamas tucked up in bed. That didn't stop Oscar talking about escaping, but I had to switch off from him, because the end of the day was my favourite time. The time when the lights are turned off and everyone is sleeping. My favourite, favourite, favourite time of all – better than playing football, better than playing *Warrior Attack*, better than anything else in the whole wide world. The time I got to talk to Luke on my own. Or, more like, he got to talk to me.

First of all we chatted about Mum and Dad, and how much we missed them. Then we talked about what had happened that day and the people we had met, and we went through them all, in my head.

Effie?
Friend.

Kaya?

Friend.

Oscar?

Not sure.

And we thought about the others: Ethan, Rhys
and Malik.

They seem okay.

Millie, Hannah, Alice and Lowrie?

*We haven't had much time to talk to them. Can
we read now?*

But we're talking about the day.

I know. But can we read The Boy, the Girl and the Lion?

I'll just check if Oscar is asleep.

I rolled over on my side. Oscar had his back turned to me, so I couldn't
tell if he was sleeping, only that for once he was quiet.

So, Tyler's brother hasn't picked him up yet?

I don't think that is going to happen.

Why not?

Because we're a long way from Brighton.

Oh.

Our book and torch were in the bottom drawer. I slid it open slowly,
without making a sound.

I read to Luke every night, and it was always the same book, *The
Boy, the Girl and the Lion*. It was the last book we read together, at

home and when he was in hospital. We'd read it over fifty times and just because we were in a different bed, miles away from home, it didn't mean we had to stop.

I pulled up my knees and tugged my duvet over myself like a tent, then turned on the torch.

Ready?
Ready.

I read our book in my head.

Once there was a boy, a girl . . .
And a lion. I love the lion. He's really funny.
Yeah, Lukey, the lion is really funny.

I smiled to myself and started reading again.

'Once there was a boy, a girl and a lion. This is the story of how they all came to meet, in the middle of the Amazon rainforest.'

Can we skip to the good part?
You always say that.
I know.
But why?
Because it annoys you.
So, shall I continue?
Yep, please. Won't do it again.

I looked at the page and got ready to start again.

'Once there was a boy, a girl and a lion. This is the story of how they –'

'Oi!'

My duvet was ripped off the bed.

Oscar was standing over me, shining the light from his phone in my face.

'I can hear you, you know!'

> He heard me.
> *He heard you!*

My head scrambled in panic. Luke had interrupted me so much I hadn't realised I'd been reading out loud.

'You could hear . . .' I stammered.

'Yeah,' he said. 'There's a girl, a boy and a lion, I get it, but can't you just read to yourself?'

He threw my duvet back on top of me.

'And don't you dare tell anyone I've got another phone.'

I sighed with relief.

> *That was close.*
> Yeah, Lukey, that was close.

AWARDS FOR HEROES

My head is full of worries as the chatter of the crowd surrounds me.

Still no Effie.

Still empty seats where she and her nan should be.

I wish I'd asked whether she had booked in when we left the hotel this morning, but breakfast and checking out with Mum and Dad was a rush of nerves. I should have got Dad to go down to the reception last night. I wish Effie had replied to my messages, but the grey tick next to them means she's not even seen them. I want to check my phone now but we were told to turn them off when we came in because the whole ceremony is being shown on TV. All I need is one message; but most of all I want Effie and her nan to walk through the side door and sit in my row.

I can't stop worrying as Dom Fox walks back onto the stage.

'So,' he says, putting his hands together. 'Let us take our minds back to that day in August. Like any serious event, it was one of those occasions when we can all remember where we were and what we were doing.'

'Yeah, too right,' whispers Oscar. 'Down a mine with half a pasty and a packet of Jelly Tots.'

I force a chuckle because it sounds funny now, but it was nowhere near funny at the time.

'I can certainly remember where I was,' continued Dom. 'Stuck with a car full of my kids, in the drive-thru at KFC.'

There's a murmur from the audience like they aren't sure if they were supposed to laugh at that or not.

'Anyway.' Dom put his hands together. 'Let's just set the scene for you. Here's a little film about Swallow Heights, and then we'll meet Trey Walcott, who is going to tell us a little bit about what they do at the centre.'

The lights dim as a film starts to play on the screen. A picture of the sea, waves crashing against the rocks, then the camera swoops across the clifftop as if attached to a seagull – silver dust, lots of silver dust, then the grey roofs of the buildings, the dorms, the toilets, the canteen, and then the mine. The camera circles it, then sweeps down – rusty brown metal against a deep blue sky. And music plays, low deep notes, getting quicker and higher, like it's an exciting TV drama. Suddenly I feel like I did the first morning. Dry dusty throat, butterflies in my stomach, surrounded by strangers, wondering why I was there, fearing what would come next. And I really want Effie.

I lean across to Oscar. 'Your phone,' I whisper. 'Did you leave it on?'

'Course.' He reaches into his pocket.

'Has she messaged?' I ask.

Oscar looks at his phone.

'Nothing,' he says. 'But the signal is rubbish in here.'

41

'Milo.' Mum taps me on the arm. 'Something wrong?'

'Nothing,' I say.

'You sure?'

'Yes, I'm sure.'

I sit back in my seat. No, I'm not sure. I'm not sure at all.

The picture changes to one of Trey wearing his cap and sunglasses, arms folded, muscles bulging out of his T-shirt, standing outside the mine.

'Welcome to Swallow Heights,' he says, exactly like he did on the first day.

'And just tell us a little bit about what you do here,' says an interviewer.

'Well,' Trey pauses, 'a number of things really. The centre can be used by companies for team-building exercises, and the general public can stay, you know, groups of friends, wedding parties, things like that. But most of the year, when the team are here, it's used for something very different.'

'Yeah,' whispers Oscar. 'A prison camp!'

The picture switches to the dorms. They look much smaller than I remember. I pick out the beds where me and Oscar slept, then the girls' dorm, which we only ever saw from the doorway.

'It's a place for children to come and stay,' says Trey, 'where they can relax and make friends, but maybe most of all, discover things about themselves. Life can be so rushed at home; some children can get lost in that. Here, well, I guess we just slow things down. If the only thing to do in the day is to climb a rockface, then that's all we do. It's about setting challenges and trying to overcome them.'

42

'And then, of course, there is the mine,' says the interviewer.

'Yes,' says Trey. 'Then there is the mine.'

The camera moves towards the window of a dorm and I see the yard, the dust, then the hill with the mine on top. And all the time the music grows louder and my stomach flips like it's got wriggling maggots inside.

The mine.

And there is the mine.

CHAPTER 4

I WISH I COULD
TALK / *ME TOO* 🙁

I worried all night that Oscar had actually heard me talking to Luke, so much that I couldn't sleep. To try to take my mind off it, I wrote a story in my diary about a boy who was lost on an iceberg in the middle of the Arctic Ocean, with only seals and penguins for company. They helped him build an igloo and search for food. Luckily for me, Luke is always quiet when I write, because he knows that if he isn't I won't have any new stories to read to him, but I made sure the penguins and seals can speak, so that Luke can do the voices. I must have written for ages because the dark was turning to grey outside by the time I'd finished. But then I still couldn't sleep because I was pretty sure there weren't any penguins in the Arctic, so I had to go back and change the penguins to polar bears.

At breakfast that morning, I was worried that Oscar would blab to all the others that he'd heard me. Then add stuff like 'You're strange' and 'What a weirdo.' But he just sat at the table like the rest of us, munching on a bacon sandwich. He didn't even ask why I was wearing my coat all the time, like kids did at school.

'So,' Sabula said, pointing at the whiteboard in front of her. 'As you can see, all your names are up here, and ours, along with a list of all the things we hope to do later in the week like Archery on Tuesday, Axe-throwing on Wednesday … Rock-climbing that afternoon, and so on … Sledging down the dust, and a trip down the mine. But today, Sunday,' she said, still pointing, 'we're going to be doing Kayaking and Zip-wire.'

There were some groans, but more *yes*es.

Sabula held her hand in the air. The noise died down.

'So, now we'll split you into groups. We will mix you all up during the week, but for now, most of you will be with the people you know. So, Alice, Lowrie and Ethan, you'll be with Trey this morning. Oscar, Effie and Milo, you'll be with Lois.'

'Yes!' Oscar nudged me in the ribs. Not only had he not said anything about my reading out loud, it seemed like he was glad we were in the same group. Maybe we had made a secret deal; he wouldn't say anything about my reading, if I didn't tell anyone about his phone, which seemed okay to me.

But Effie didn't look so pleased.

'Should have known,' she said. 'The most annoying boy here, and I get stuck with him.'

'Thanks,' I said.

Effie rolled her eyes. 'You know I mean him.' She nodded at Oscar, who was helping load the red life jackets into the minibus. 'He's like a bumblebee,' she said. 'Buzzes everywhere, then hits you with a sting.'

That's a good one.

I chuckled.

'But he is, isn't he?' Effie continued. 'Just do me a favour, Milo, and sit next to me. They said it's only a ten-minute ride, but that's ten minutes too long ... You don't have to talk. Just sit there and block him off.'

I thought maybe Effie was being a bit mean, but she was right, he was a bit of a bumblebee, which was okay as long as he didn't sting me. Effie sighed with relief as Oscar sat down across the aisle from us. I tried to think of something to say, but suddenly Luke was kicking off in my head like he'd only just worked out that a kayak goes on water.

Milo, we can't do this.
Of course, we can.
But I can't swim.
You'll be okay, you're with me.
Still don't want to ... I know! I know!

I jumped in my seat.

Effie glanced at me.

I smiled then looked ahead as the minibus drove on.

You did it again.
Sorry ... But I got the answer.
To what?
Going in a kayak.

46

What's that?

How about we wear arm—

'No!' I said out loud. 'We are not wearing armbands!'

'Armbands!' Oscar laughed. 'You want to wear armbands?'

'No.' My face burned as everyone turned round. 'I said, we're *not* wearing armbands.'

Aww!

'Because we've got life jackets.'

Oscar gave me a *You're weird* look; exactly the look I'd feared him giving me at breakfast. Effie raised her left eyebrow, which is kind of the same thing.

I looked ahead, trying to ignore everyone else as the minibus turned down a narrow lane.

Are life jackets better than armbands?

I took a deep breath.

Are they?

Yes.

And maybe my coat will help.

It might.

. . . Wish I'd learned to swim.

Me too.

47

I sighed and rested my chin on my rucksack. A memory of Mum and Dad popped into my head, at the swimming pool encouraging Luke to let go of the sides. He was shivering from fright and the cold. 'Maybe wait a while,' said Dad. 'After all, Milo didn't learn until he was seven.'

'Yeah.' Luke had climbed back onto the side. 'Wait until I'm seven, like Milo. I'll do it then. For now I'll just practise up here.'

I smiled at the memory of his cheeky grin. And I smiled even more as I remembered Mum and Dad laughing as Luke walked around the edge of the pool waving his arms like an octopus stranded on land.

I wished Luke could swim. But most of all, I wished he'd made it to be seven.

'I didn't want to do it anyway,' Oscar said, as we ate lunch afterwards in the shade of the mine. 'Who wants to sit in a piece of plastic on the sea?'

'You're only saying that because you went round in circles,' said Effie.

'At least I went out and didn't just sit on the beach and watch.'

'Maybe *I* just didn't want to do it,' snapped Effie, defensively.

'Yeah, and maybe I just wanted to go round in circles ... Anyway, why are you getting so stroppy?'

'I'm not,' said Effie, tugging at her hair. 'Just saying. Besides, it's not like they told us we had to do everything.'

'Yeah, right,' said Oscar turning away. For a moment I thought he was going to stop being argumentative but as I'd feared all he was doing was switching his target from Effie to me.

'And what about you?' he said pointing at me.

My heart skipped.

'What about Milo?' asked Effie.

'Am I the only one who noticed he spun so quickly it was like he was going down a plughole?' said Oscar.

Everyone on our table laughed, and I had to laugh too, because after being scared of the water, it turned out Luke loved being in a kayak. It was only that he was talking so much that he got me confused with my left and right.

'I lost control.'

'Just a bit,' said Matty, as he came over with a fresh jug of water. 'But you did okay in the end ... once you got straight. At one point we all thought you were headed towards France.'

I smiled, even though I couldn't tell him the reason I'd gone round in circles.

'Okay,' said Trey, wiping his forehead on his sleeve. 'Listen, it is very hot, and the forecast says it's going to get hotter during the week, so maybe we'll try and get some breeze and do the zip-wire this afternoon, after all.'

'Yes!' Oscar clenched his fist.

Yes! That was Luke.

'Yes!' That was just about everyone else.

I glanced up at the zip-wire on top of the hill. Dad had said it was the highest and longest in Europe.

It's going to be amazing, Milo.
Yeah, amazingly high and amazingly long.

49

Luke had just overcome his fear of water; I was nowhere near ready to overcome my fear of heights.

Effie put her hand on my shoulder like she knew I was worried.

'You'll be okay,' she said. 'I went on the one at Blackpool with my nan and she hates heights.'

I smiled.

Ask her how. Go on.

'Aren't you going to ask how I made her do it?'

'Yeah,' I said. 'Sorry.'

'It's okay,' she said. 'We can't all be as gobby as him.' She nodded at Oscar. 'Anyway,' she looked back at me, 'it was quite easy. I told her she wasn't scared of heights; she was scared of falling.'

How did that help?

'How did that help?'

You're getting better at this.
Thanks.

'Don't know.' Effie grinned. 'All I know is that she closed her eyes.'

I laughed. 'What,' I said, 'all the way down?'

'Pretty much,' said Effie, 'until the man at the bottom caught her. And she didn't mind that bit, because he looked like Freddy Belling, this celebrity cook on the telly.'

'Your nan sounds nice,' I said.

'She is,' said Effie. 'She's the best. She does loads of things that make me laugh or makes up words that don't actually mean anything.'

'Like what?' I asked.

'Like *confloption*.' Effie smiled. 'She always says that when something goes wrong or is a mess. I thought it was a Welsh word at first, but she made it up. Like Oscar's spiked-up hair.' She nodded at Oscar who was talking with Alice and Trey as they filled their bottles at the tap. 'His hair would be a confloption.'

I laughed.

'It's a good word,' I said.

'Yeah.' Effie chuckled. 'I could think of lots of others for him.'

'Don't you like him?' I asked.

Effie shrugged. 'He's just so annoying; look at him. It's like he thinks no one knows what he's up to.'

'How do you mean?' I looked back at Oscar, who was now nodding his head like he was deep in conversation with Trey. For someone who said he wouldn't talk to the instructors the night before, he seemed to be doing it non-stop.

'It's his plan,' Effie said quietly. 'He reckons that if he keeps talking it won't give them time and space to ask questions.'

'Not a bad plan,' I said.

'No,' said Effie. 'It's that or he's just trying to hide that he's as scared of heights as you are. You really don't want to go on it, do you?'

51

I do! I do!
I don't.

'Not sure, really.'

Effie laughed.

'Well, you took a long time to decide that.'

'Yeah.' I smiled. 'I guess I did.'

Effie looked at me like she was trying to work out what I was thinking. I wondered if Oscar had spoken to her about hearing me the night before.

I lifted up my water bottle. 'Suppose we'd better fill these,' I said, hoping that would stop her looking, but I could still feel her eyes on me as we headed to the tap. Maybe I should learn from Oscar and ask questions to stop people trying to find out more about me. But after months of being quiet, it was hard to know how to start.

It's easy.
It used to be. Now I don't know what to say. It's much easier talking to you.
Just ask her about her nan. She likes talking about her nan.
Okay.

'Is it far?' I said.

Effie looked at the tap, then back at me.

'It's just there, Milo.'

52

'No,' I said, scrambling for words. 'I meant your nan's, is it far to go when you visit?'

'Oh, I don't visit,' she said. 'I live with her. Always have. Just me and her.'

'Oh, sorry,' I said.

'What for? I'm not.'

I looked down at my bottle, wondering where her mum and dad were. It was like the *D*-word was hanging in the air, just like after Luke went ... The horrible silence with teachers at school, with my aunties and uncles when they visited ... They couldn't say the *D*-word and they hardly ever said his name. They definitely never put both in the same sentence. And now here I was doing it to Effie, and that made me as bad as them.

So we should say something ... I think we should say something.
Yeah.

'Milo?'

I looked up and saw Effie looking right at me.

'Yeah?'

'It's going all over your trainers.'

Oops!

I looked down at the water splashing over my feet.

Effie turned the tap off and looked across the dust.

'Think we'd better catch up with the others,' she said.

'Yeah,' I said. 'Sorry.'

Effie smiled.

'It's okay,' she said. 'I just thought you were trying to get out of the zip-wire.'

No way. No way.

'No way,' I said.

She laughed.

'Milo, can I ask you something?'

Here we go!

'Yeah.'

'Are you quiet because you want to be, or because you don't know what to say?'

I don't understand. Do you understand?

I shrugged.

'I don't know,' I said. 'I suppose it's because I want to be. I mean, there are lots of things I want to say, but I just say them in my head. My mum said I used to talk so much that she couldn't shut me up, and now she wishes she'd never said that.'

'What made you stop talking?'

'I don't know,' I said. 'Stuff.'

Stuff?

'I guess that's why we're here,' said Effie. 'Because of . . . stuff.'

'Yeah,' I sighed. 'I guess it is.'

As we followed the rest of the group up the hill towards the zip-wire, I couldn't stop thinking about my conversation with Effie. For a moment I'd felt like telling her about Luke, and what had happened, but it had been locked inside me for so long that it was like I'd lost the key to let it out.

But I didn't want to find the key. I was happy that Luke was locked inside me. Although sometimes it would have been nice to have a break, just for a while, and one of those times was when I was at the top of the tower, waiting to go down the zip-wire.

Oh, look, we can see the mountains . . . And the ocean.

I know, I know, but I don't want to look.

But it's amazing!

Not amazing. Really not amazing.

I gripped the metal handrail.

I can see Oscar and the others at the bottom. They look like ants. Can we wave? Let's wave.

No!

My legs trembled as Matty waited for me at the top.

'You'll be okay, Milo,' he said, strapping me into a harness. 'It looks way worse than it is. Jumping off is the hardest part.'

'Yeah,' I said. My voice shook with my body.

'This secures you to the wire.' Matty lifted up a metal hook and looped it over the wire. 'Just pop your hands through the straps,' he said.

I closed my eyes.

We can do it! We can do it!

'You'll be okay, Milo.' That was Effie standing behind me.

'Yes,' said Lois. 'You're even taller than I am, and if I can do it, I'm sure you can.'

Yeah, you'll be okay.

But I didn't feel okay. The website said the zip-wire was a thousand metres long, but it looked like miles to me. Trey and the others had said we had to rise to the challenge, and we'd learn about ourselves, but all I had learned about myself was that I really did hate heights and that I wanted to pee.

But we won't.
No.
Because that would be embarrassing. Like when you did on your first day at school.
Okay, I don't think we need to mention that now.
Sorry.

The wind whistled across the wire as Matty's walkie-talkie crackled.

'All good here, send the next one down.'

I shook my head. Matty bent down in front of me. 'Milo,' he said, 'you don't have to do it. Sometimes the bravest thing to do is say no.'

'I'm not sure.'

I am!

'Part of me wants to stay here,' I said. 'But the other part of me wants to jump.'

Matty smiled. 'Well, yeah,' he said. 'We all have that inner voice.'

'Do we?'

'Yeah, course.' Matty looked surprised that I doubted him, but not as surprised as I was that he had an inner voice too. 'It's just how much we decide to listen to it.'

His walkie-talkie crackled as the wind blew around us.

'Everything okay, mate?' I recognised Trey's voice and realised he was the person waving to us from the bottom. 'Only we're clear down here.'

'Yeah, all good,' Matty said as he waved to Trey, then looked back at me. 'We can unhook you and chat about it now,' he said turning back to me.

'Yes,' said Lois. 'We can do it now, or when you've reached the bottom.'

They want you to talk about me.

I know.

But Oscar said we can't.

'You'll be fine, Milo.' That was Effie, again, like she knew what Loi
and Matty were trying to do. 'Just remember my nan.'

I put my hands through the straps.

'It's okay,' I said. 'I think I can do it now.'

Lois and Matty smiled.

'See,' Matty said. 'That's what happens when you listen to tha
voice. Unless of course it was Effie.'

I smiled nervously. There were so many voices talking but the onl
one that mattered was Luke in my head, yelling, *Let's go! Let's go!*

Matty pressed a button on his walkie-talkie. 'Coming dow
now,' he said.

I looked down. My toes were poking over the edge even though
couldn't remember moving my legs.

I gripped tight on the straps.

Aaaaaaaaaaaaaaaaaaaaaarh!
Geronimoooooooooooooooooo!

CHAPTER 5

THE CLOCK GAME /
WE ZIP OUR LIPS

My heart was still thudding from the zip-wire as we ate tea that evening. Oscar was reliving every single ride, like he'd discovered something different each time, but all I'd noticed, once I had opened my eyes, was how quickly it felt you were going if you looked at the ground, and how slow it felt when you looked at the sky.

It was brilliant . . . Brilliant, brilliant, brilliant.
Okay, it was brilliant.

I put some chips in my mouth, hoping Luke would at least let me eat in peace, but he was still going, *Brilliant, brilliant, brilliant,* when Oscar leaned across the table and whispered –

'I'm going to sneak back up tonight.' Burger crumbs flew from his mouth. '. . . anyone want to come? Take some more pictures.' He slid his phone out of his pocket. 'Who wants to see the video I took on the way down?'

'You so did not,' said Effie, disbelievingly.

'So did,' said Oscar.

He checked across the room to the table where Sabula, Trey and the other instructors were sitting. 'I sent it to Tyler, because he keeps sending me videos of him and my other mates doing tricks on their skateboards on the precinct. This is way better than that.'

'Prove it,' said Effie.

'I will,' said Oscar. 'But don't crowd round or they'll see us ... I'll show you lot later, yeah.' He waved the rest of the group away. 'Probably won't, though,' Oscar said under his breath. 'We'll just keep it to us.'

> *Bit mean.*
> A bit.

'What?' Oscar said like he knew the thoughts going through my head. 'You want them to be in our group?'

I shrugged. 'I didn't know we had a group.'

Oscar shook his head like I didn't make any sense. 'I don't know what Kaya and Malik are doing here, anyway. They're so posh.'

'And posh kids can't have problems?' said Effie.

'What problems can they have? Did you see, one of their parents had a Range Rover? Must be loaded.'

'And you're not?' Effie laughed. 'I mean, you got brand-new Nike trainers and the newest iPhone you can get.'

'Well, yeah,' said Oscar, looking down at his trainers, like he'd forgotten he had them. 'But that doesn't mean anything.'

'You just said it did,' said Effie. 'You said being rich meant you couldn't have problems.'

'I dunno.' Oscar shrugged as he kicked at the dust. 'Dunno what I meant. You're confusing me.'

Effie glanced at me, like she wondered if she should keep going, but from the way Oscar had reacted it seemed she had prodded a sore spot that he didn't want to talk about. And I knew how that felt.

'Come on, Milo,' said Oscar, nudging me. 'If she doesn't want to watch with us, that's up to her.'

'I do,' said Effie. 'You're just being too sensitive.'

I expected Oscar to snap, but it was like he didn't want to continue the discussion any longer. Instead, he just looked at his phone in the palm of his hand.

'I've turned the sound down, obvs,' he said.

'Just play it, Oscar,' said Effie.

On the screen was a close-up of Oscar's face with his yellow hard hat on. His eyes were bulging and his mouth was open so wide you could almost see his tonsils.

'That's useless,' said Effie, 'We can't see anything. It's like you filmed your reflection on the back of a spoon.'

'It gets better,' said Oscar. 'Just wait.' He pressed play.

'Argh! Argh!' The sound was down low but I could still hear Oscar screaming on the screen, even though all we could see was his face.

'That so isn't on the zip-wire,' said Effie.

'It is,' said Oscar.

'Okay, then, how did you put the phone back in your pocket before you got to the bottom?'

61

'Easy,' said Oscar. 'I just di—'

The screen changed from Oscar's face to a white sink.

Effie burst out laughing.

'Oh, wait!' Oscar fumbled for the stop as a fake 'Argh! Argh!' played from his phone. 'That's the wrong ... I mean, that was after.'

'You filmed it in the boys' toilet.' Effie's eyes watered. 'Oscar, you weren't even outside!'

I couldn't stop myself laughing, because Effie was laughing too.

Oscar's face turned red.

'It's not that funny,' he said. 'It sounded better in there, and I don't know why you're laughing.' He turned to me. 'It's not like you even say anything. The only time you do is when you read out loud to yourself.'

Bit mean.

Very mean.

Oscar had finally snapped and I couldn't think of a reply, but Effie could.

'What are you picking on Milo for?' said Effie. 'It's got nothing to do with him.'

'It has,' said Oscar. 'Like, who reads out loud to themselves? I was six when I stopped that.'

Bit rude, too. Say something. Go on, Milo. Tell him it's none of his business. No, tell him he's got big ears. Tell him his hair looks like a toilet brush.

62

'You've got big ears,' I blurted.

Oscar stopped dead.

'What?'

'And your hair looks like a toilet brush.'

Effie put her hand over her mouth, trying to stop more laughter coming out, but I could hear Luke's chuckle like he was there in the room.

Oscar held his hand up to his hair. 'Does not,' he said, pulling at it. 'And my ears are okay, aren't they?'

'I'm sorry,' I said. 'That just came out. I really meant to say, you don't know why I read like that.'

'So why do you?'

'Everything okay here?' Matty put his hands on the table and leaned over like teachers do at school.

Effie stopped laughing. Oscar had one hand up to his ear like he was trying to flatten it down. I slid my hand over his phone on the table.

He was being horrible.

I know, but he was going to get into trouble.

'Yeah.' Oscar glanced at me. He still looked angry but he'd noticed what I'd done. 'We're okay.'

'Good,' said Matty. 'Only maybe you should all save your words, as we're getting ready to play the clock game.'

'What, now?' Oscar's face dropped like he'd just been told he could never go on a zip-wire again. 'Do we have to?'

'You don't "have" to,' said Matty. 'But it would be good if you did

I looked across the room. While we had been arguing, all the other
had arranged the chairs into a circle.

'What's wrong?' asked Effie.

'The clock game,' said Oscar, nodding at the chairs. 'I should have
known. They're doing the clock game again.'

'What's that?'

The three of us had just kind of fallen out, but it was like fear o
what was going to happen next had brought us back together again.

'You're about to find out,' Oscar sighed. 'But you don't want t
be number six. In fact, you don't want to be any number, so I'm off

'Oscar! Not so fast.' Trey held out his arm.

'No,' said Oscar, 'I'm out of here.'

Uh-oh.
Shush.

'What do you mean,' Trey laughed, 'you're out of here?'

'I mean, I know what you're doing,' said Oscar, turning away.

'What's up?' Sabula walked over.

'Him,' said Oscar. 'In fact, all of you. You're all nice, nice, nice
then bam! You get us talking about ourselves.'

That's okay, we like talking 😊

'Well,' said Sabula, 'I'm not sure it's like that. I mean, we'll all tak
it in turns, even the adults, and besides, is talking really a bad thing

We're only going to talk about the things we did today, just like anyone does. And if you really don't want to then you can just write it in your diary. No one has to see that.'

> *Oh, we've got a diary . . . Can we show them*
> *your stories?*
> No.
> *Go on, let them see the one about the boy on*
> *the iceberg.*
> It's not finished. Besides, diaries are personal.
> *Like a secret?*
> Yes, Lukey, like one big secret.

Oscar puffed out his cheeks.

'Okay,' he said. 'Then I'll stay. But I'm not sitting anywhere near him.' He nodded at Matty.

Sabula smiled. 'That's fine,' she said. 'So just sit where you want.'

'How about here?' said Trey, standing behind a chair by the radiator with the boys and girls in his group. 'You can have the twelve o'clock seat, Oscar.'

Oscar ignored him and walked across to the chair at three o'clock. He glanced at me and Effie like we should follow him. I sat at four o'clock, Effie sat at five, then the rest of the group filled in the gaps between her and Sabula who was sat at nine.

'Okay,' said Trey as he placed a giant clock hand on the floor. 'Like you might have heard me saying to Oscar, this isn't about us trying

65

to catch you out, it's just all of us having the chance to get to know each other.'

Oscar nudged me, then leaned towards me.

'Make it up,' he whispered.

What?

'What?'

Oscar leaned closer. 'Make it up. Say anything, as long as it's not the truth.'

'What's that?' asked Trey.

'Nothing,' said Oscar, grinning. 'Just saying this better be good.'

I sat back in my chair wondering what he meant by *not the truth*.

Does he know about me?

Did he know?

I'd spent the last few months wondering if anyone knew about us. But Trey couldn't have. We'd only known him a day. We'd only made two mistakes, and they were so small that no one could have noticed.

'So,' said Sabula, 'who would like to start? It's very simple, really. Just say one thing you liked about the day, and why. Then, once you've done that, that person gets to spin the hand on the clock.'

We all looked at one another. It was just like on the first day when no one wanted to introduce themselves.

66

I—

Don't even think about it!

I was just going to ask if we could spin the hand.

No, let's just sit still.

I sat on my hands. It was seven o'clock and the film was going to start at eight. There were twelve of us and if everyone spoke for more than five minutes, if we were really lucky, they might run out of time before it got to us three. And though Oscar, Effie and I knew each other better, from the way everyone else squirmed in their chairs, I guessed they were thinking the same.

'Okay,' said Sabula. 'Anyone?'

We all stared at the clock hand.

'Not to worry,' said Sabula, 'we'll all get to go, but we'll let the hand choose.'

'Okay, I'll go first.' Effie raised her hand.

Oscar leaned forward and looked at her wide-eyed like he was trying to tell her she'd made one big mistake.

'Best to get it over with.' She shrugged. 'Besides, it's no big deal.'

But it is. It is.

I fidgeted in my chair, like a combination of Oscar's look and my unease might get Effie to change her mind.

'Well done, Effie,' said Sabula. 'So, it's quite simple: something you did and something you realised about yourself.'

'Okay.' Effie glanced at me. 'Well, it's not really something I did, but it sort of was.'

What's she going to say?
Hang on.

'I guess I learned that I can give people the confidence to do something,' said Effie. 'Milo really didn't want to go on the zip-wire, but I told him it was okay.'

'Yes, brilliant,' Oscar whispered under his breath. 'Deflection: avoid talking about yourself by talking about someone else.'

'Oscar!' Trey glared.

Oscar shrugged. 'Just saying.'

'Go on, Effie,' Trey said, looking back at her. 'What were you saying?'

'I just told him he'd be okay,' Effie said, smiling at me.

'Excellent,' said Trey. 'And how did you feel when you saw Milo going off down the mountain?'

'Good,' she said. 'But at first I was a bit worried because he sounded so excited and scared at the same time.'

That was you.
It was you!

'I think we all heard it,' said Oscar. 'It sounded like someone was strangling a cat.'

Everyone laughed.

Ha! Ha!

'It's okay, Milo,' said Trey. 'No need to look so worried. You did it, after all.'

'I know.' I glanced at Effie. 'It was because she said her nan had done it.'

'Well, good on Nan,' said Sabula.

'Yes,' said Effie. 'She's brilliant. The best.'

Oscar bent down and fiddled with a shoelace that was already tied.

'Tell her to stop,' he whispered urgently. 'It's a trap.'

'So, tell us a little bit about your nan,' said Sabula.

'There,' said Oscar. 'Told you.'

'That's it, really,' said Effie. 'She does everything with me.'

'Like what?'

'Well, go to town together at the weekends, and she takes me to the cinema in Rhyl, even when she tells me she thinks she's too old for some of the films.'

'What do you say, when she says that?'

Effie shrugged. 'I just tell her she's my nan and that I don't care what everybody else thinks. She's not just my nan, she's my best friend and I like being with her all the time.'

Where's her mum and dad?
Shush!
Oh, is it the D-word?
I don't know.
Then ask her. Ask her where her mum and dad are.

69

'Where's your mum and dad?' I blurted.

Everyone looked at me. I was sat at four o'clock, but it felt like I was smack bang in the middle of the clockface.

'Sorry,' I mumbled. 'That wasn't supposed to come out. I just . . .'

'It's okay,' said Effie. 'I don't mind.'

'So where are they, then?' asked Oscar.

'Oh.' Effie shrugged like she was about to say something totally unimportant.

'Maybe we should stop now,' said Sabula. 'Have a vote on a film.'

Yes! Spidey, Spidey, Spidey.

'No, it's okay,' said Effie.

'So where are they, then?'

'Oh, they're dead.'

'Wow!' Oscar sat back in his chair, a hand on his head. 'There,' he said to Trey. 'Are you happy now?'

I looked at Effie, checking if she was okay, but she just stared ahead at the clock hand.

I think she's going to cry. Can we hug her?
I'm not sure.
Can we spin the hand, then?
–

I glanced at the others. They all had sad looks on their faces like they were the ones who'd lost their parents. Sabula stood up and walked

70

over to Effie, like she knew what had just happened. Which she probably did. All the instructors must have known why each of us was here. How else could they try to help us if they didn't know what was wrong in the first place? Or was it their job to find out our problems?

Sabula put her arm around Effie and led her away from the group. Trey picked up the spinner.

Wait, it's our turn. Milo, tell him it's our turn.

I shook my head.

No, Lukey, I don't think we're playing that game any more.

CHAPTER 6

PUSHING BUTTONS /
WE TALK TO EFFIE

Everyone was talking in whispers as we got into our pyjamas, ready for the film. We were all talking about Effie. Oscar kept blaming Trey, saying that he was right all along about the clock game, that the instructors always get you to say something you don't want to. But as I replayed the game in my head, it felt like Oscar was the one who had made her say it, not anyone else.

I managed to sit next to Effie during *Iron Man 3*.

> *Still no Spidey.*
> I tried.
> *We should get two votes!*
> True.

As Iron Man flew around the screen, I wanted to tell Effie I was sorry about her mum and dad but the sound of the explosions was so loud that I would have had to shout and I was scared that if the sound suddenly stopped, the word 'dead' would have echoed around the hut.

I tried to talk to her during a break. I wanted to help her like she'd helped me on the zip-wire. I went and got us crisps and a drink, but by the time I got back to my seat she was walking out of the hut with Alice.

'Girls,' said Oscar, taking her drink from me. 'Why do they do that?'

'Do what?' I asked.

'Go to the toilet together. My sister does it with her friends. I don't do it.'

We do.

It's not the same.

'Weird,' said Oscar.

'Yeah,' I said. 'Weird.'

'But do you think she's okay?' Oscar said, checking over his shoulder. 'I mean, I knew something was up, but she just blurted it out, like she was answering a question in Maths.'

'Yeah,' I said. 'I know, but not all people are the same. Maybe she's putting on a brave face, like she doesn't care but –'

'Shush,' said Oscar. 'She's coming back. Talk later, yeah.' He shuffled along a seat to let Effie sit between us.

'Here,' he said, holding out the drink. 'I had a sip, but I won't be offended if you switch the straw round. Oh, and you can have these too if you want.' He pulled a wrinkled packet of wine gums out of his pocket.

Ooh, wine gums.

Effie scrunched up her nose.

'No, thanks,' she said.

We'll have them. Any red ones? I like the red ones.

'No, really,' said Oscar. 'I want you to have them.'

Effie shook her head.

'Oscar,' she said. 'I am okay. You don't have to pretend to be nice. But if you insist, I'll give them to Milo.'

Yes! Cool!

'Cool.'

'Cool?' Effie gave me a weird look. 'It's just wine gums, Milo.'

Argh! They're all green!

'Yeah,' I said, shoving them in my mouth. 'I know.'

Bit mean.
Sorry.

It was mean but I couldn't help grinning to myself as the film started again.

Luke always did love red gums.

In my head I promised him that I'd get another packet from the vending machine outside the canteen if there was a break.

In a quiet bit, when Iron Man was trying out a new gadget, I finally got to talk to Effie.

'Are you okay?' I asked.

'What about?' she replied.

'Well, you know.'

'Oh, my parents,' she said, waving me away. 'I'm used to it now. They only died once but I must have told people a thousand times.'

I didn't know what to say, so I just looked back at the screen. How could she just dismiss people dying like that, like she didn't care? It had only taken a moment for Luke to slip away, but I felt like I was going to hurt for the rest of my life.

Effie chuckled as Iron Man made a joke and she laughed out loud when he splatted Killian against a brick wall.

Maybe she was putting on a brave face, but her brave face was very weird. All through the rest of the film I kept glancing around the room, at the silhouettes of the heads in front of me, at the lit-up faces of the kids behind. I wondered if they all had something they were trying to hide.

CHAPTER 7

BUTTONS / *THE BOY ON THE ICEBERG*

'Buttons,' Oscar whispered as he got ready for bed that evening while the other boys were reading on their beds or playing cards. 'They know how to press our buttons, how to make us talk, or get angry.'

'Then why do you let them?' I asked as I held my pen over a page in my diary, trying to finish the story about the boy on an iceberg.

'I don't know,' replied Oscar. 'I can't help it. It's like one minute I'm okay, the next my head explodes. Do you know what I mean? Does anyone push your buttons?'

'Well . . .' I paused.

> *I do not!*
> *Do I?*
> No, Luke, not really.
> *Do you think I would push Oscar's buttons?*

'Oh, definitely!' I laughed.

76

'What's that?' asked Oscar, sitting down on his bed.

'Definitely . . .' My thoughts scrambled in my head. 'Definitely not,' I said. 'No one pushes my buttons.'

Oscar shook his head. 'You know, you can be a bit weird, sometimes.'

Uh-oh.

'Can I?'

'Yeah, I mean, you're quiet and stuff, but it's not just that, it's like you're not concentrating or something.'

I shrugged. 'Just writing, I guess.'

'No,' said Oscar, 'it's not just when you're doing that, it's most of the time . . . Anyway, you wait, they'll push your buttons. They always find a way, just like they did with Effie. I bet you thought she was "normal". I know I did, but it turns out she's got secrets like the rest of us.'

'Yeah,' I said. 'Only it's not a secret any more.'

'True,' said Oscar, checking around the room. Most of the others were quiet, but James, Malik and Sam were playing *Top Trumps* in the corner. 'So,' Oscar turned back to me, 'what's yours? You never said.'

Uh-oh.

'I did,' I replied. 'I said there wasn't anything. Besides, it wouldn't be a secret any more if I told you.'

'Ah.' Oscar swung his legs over the side of his bed. 'So there is something, then.'

I stared at my diary, pretending I was reading.

Oscar leaned towards me, so close I could smell popcorn on his breath.

'Go on, Milo,' he whispered. 'You can tell me. Is it in there?' He nodded at my diary.

'No,' I said.

'Let me look.' Oscar reached out. I pulled my diary away and held it tight against my chest.

'Ooh,' said Oscar. 'So it *is* in there?'

'It's not,' I said. 'These are just stories. Some of the things people do and say in the day. Other stuff I just make up. Just notes,' I said. 'Like things people say, and sometimes things about how I feel.'

'Then read me some.'

'No,' I said, sliding my diary under my pillow. 'I feel tired and I want to go to sleep.'

'Ah, suit yourself.' Oscar climbed into his bed and pulled his duvet up to his chin. 'Probably just boring stuff anyway.'

'Everything okay, you two?'

I spun around and saw Matty standing in the doorway.

'Just thought I'd come and check on you all,' he said. 'And I'm afraid it's lights out. James, Malik, Sam, can you put the cards away?'

'But we're in the middle of a game,' said Malik.

'Then just keep the cards on the bedside table, and tomorrow you can pick up where you left off. We've got an early start . . . Milo, you too.' Matty nodded in my direction.

I put my notebook on my bedside table and lay back on my bed.

'Lights going out . . . Now.' The room plunged into darkness and I listened to Matty's footsteps fade away.

'Miss you already!'

'I heard that, Oscar!'

I rolled over on my side. Oscar was still convinced that the instructors were here to catch us out. They were just like teachers. If Oscar kicked off at school, he'd get told off, maybe sent out of the classroom until he'd calmed down. He said the same would happen to me if I misbehaved, but I hadn't. And I definitely hadn't at school.

I just wasn't 'myself' after Luke had gone. That's what I'd overheard Mrs Drake say after I'd been sent to the school office. Before going in I'd stopped outside the door while they were talking inside. 'His hand used to shoot up to answer every question when I took him for Maths, but now he just sits still. It's like he's not there, if you know what I mean. And it's not just Maths, it's most lessons. I thought it better that we talk instead of letting him see it in his reports.'

'Thank you,' Mum had said. 'But you're right, he's the same at home when he's watching TV, so quiet and still. The only time he's engaged is when he's watching Spider-Man movies on repeat.'

'It must be very hard, but we are here to help, to support. Perhaps –'

I never found out what the 'perhaps' was because the school secretary started using the photocopier and I thought I'd better open the door. But the trouble is, it's hard to concentrate on any subject—

When I'm here all the time?

Yeah, just a bit.

So ... can we read?

Ha, I wondered where you were.

79

Always here, Milo. So can we read your new story
about the boy on the iceberg?
It's not finished, Lukey, and I've got to get up early.
Just a little one.
Okay, once upon a time there were three little pigs . . .
Noooo! I'm too old for that!
I chuckled.

'Is that you reading again?' asked Oscar.

'No,' I said. 'I was just laughing to myself about the zip-wire.'

'Ha, yeah,' Oscar laughed. 'It was fun. I just wish we didn't have
to do all the other stuff. You know, the talking stuff.'

'Yeah,' I sighed.

'By the way.' I heard the mattress springs ping as Oscar turned over
in his bed. 'Thanks for not saying anything about my phone.'

'That's okay.'

'Got to stick together, yeah?'

'Yeah,' I sighed. 'I guess we do.'

I stared up at the ceiling. Sometimes Oscar made me laugh, and
sometimes he scared me. But he always confused me. And Effie
confused me too. How could she be so cold about her parents? But
then maybe I confused them. Maybe that's why we were all here: we
were all confused.

Mum and Dad had told me that camp was supposed to help, to get me
out of my room, to stop me thinking so much about Luke. 'Luke wouldn't
want you to be like this,' they used to say. 'Luke would want you to
remember him, but he'd also want you to get on with your own life.'

I do.

I know, but when somebody dies, they leave a space in
the seat where they used to sit and watch TV.

And they leave a space at the table where they
used to eat.

And they leave a space in the bed where they
used to sleep.

And they leave an empty space in the middle of your
chest, right here.

Wrong side, Lukey.

What?

The heart is on the left, not the right.

Oh, I always get them confused.

Yes, you do.

. . . So, is there no story tonight?

No, do you mind?

No. Is it because I make you tired?

Yeah, just a bit.

losed my eyes and thought about the next day, Monday, and all the
ngs written on the whiteboard that we had to do for the rest of the
ek. I had five more days of wondering why I was here. If Oscar was
ht, that meant five more days of the instructors trying to find out our
rets. I wasn't going to let them find out mine. No one could know I
s talking to Lukey, not Mum or Dad, or my teachers, and definitely
t Oscar or any of the instructors. They'd think I was broken and
y were the ones who could fix me.

How?

I don't know. But I'm just scared what would happen if they knew I was talking to you.

They wouldn't take me away, would they?

No. Never.

But could it be that? Could it?

It might be, Lukey. It might. But don't worry. I'll look after you.

Like you always do.

Yeah, like I always do.

I took a deep breath, then another, but it was like the air was too thick to breathe. I rolled back onto my side and tried to get me comfortable.

Do you want me to go to sleep now?

Yeah, please.

Okay. Love you.

Love you too, Lukey.

I breathed again, as love you, love you, love you, played over and over in my head. I held my hand against my chest, like it would help me keep calm, but all I felt was an ache where my heart used to be

AWARDS FOR HEROES

he audience is clapping, because a man who was walking from John
'Groats to Land's End at the time everything happened has just
onated all the money he raised – £6,863 – to the Swallow Heights
narity. And now he's standing behind a giant cheque that's being held
y Dom Fox and Carly Wyatt.

'Well, what a lovely gesture, Graham,' says Dom.

'It's the least I could do.' Graham smiles. 'When I heard what was
appening, like you, like all the country, the survival of everyone
own there was the only thing on my mind.'

'Indeed,' says Dom, putting his hand on Graham's shoulder.
Graham Gould everyone! A wonderful gesture – a lot of miles with
lenty of smiles.'

The audience claps louder and some people even whistle as Dom
uts his arm around Graham and walks him off the stage. Everyone is
miley and happy, like the show is for fun. But it's not fun. Being stuck
own there wasn't fun, and it seems Carly Wyatt knows, because she

raises her hand for the applause to stop, then looks right into a camera, her expression serious.

'Well,' she says. 'We've just heard how the events that day affected a stranger, one of us, if you like. But of course there were people far more connected to the incident.' Carly looks up at the giant screen, where a woman about the same age as my gran is sitting in her lounge chair. At the bottom of the screen, the writing says *Doreen Parson (Grandmother of Effie)*. I saw her when she dropped Effie off the camp, but Effie had told me so much about her gran that when she smiled on the screen, it was like I already knew her.

'I was clearing my desk at work when the police called,' she says. 'I don't recall the name of the person, only that he was from Devon and Cornwall Police. I knew immediately something was wrong. It's like you have a kind of sixth sense when you think one of your family is in danger, especially if it's your granddaughter. All you want to do is drop everything and get to wherever they are. But you know, it's the silliest thing, I started to think of all the stuff I needed to do, like meet my friend after work, cook tea, walk the dog.'

The audience laughed.

'Your brain does the weirdest things. Why would it do that, when all the while my Effie was in so much trouble, two hundred miles away?

I glance at my watch. Effie should be here, watching this, but she's not. What can have happened to her? The counsellor said it's normal to worry, that when you've lost one person you love in your life, you're always scared of losing another. It's why I sit at the window like a dog when Mum pops to the shops. It's why I jump every time my phone buzzes with a message. It's why I sleep with the light on. But this is the worst I've felt in a long time . . . two empty seats in the dark.

Effie and her nan. And I feel bad because Effie's nan seems lovely on the screen, but all I care about is Effie. I look up from the seats and see Oscar looking right at me, holding up his phone.

'She's messaged?'

'No, sorry, still nothing.'

I try to slow my breath.

> Luke, please tell me a chicken joke. I'll laugh. I promise
> I'll laugh.

But there's no Luke . . . and no joke.

I look back at the stage.

Please, Effie. Please get here soon.

CHAPTER 8

DUST / *LOTS OF DUST*

Like on the first day, there was a whiteboard at the end of the table
the next morning. Everything looked the same except Kayaking and
Zip-wire had been crossed through, and instead of Lois, Matty was
now in charge of our group.

'We need to watch out,' said Oscar. 'It's obvious they've put him
with us for a reason.'

'Could just be they mix it up,' said Effie.

'No.' Oscar shook his head. 'You wait,' he said. 'He'll be after one
of us. Probably not you, though.' He nodded at Effie. 'I reckon they
got all they wanted from you last night.'

'I didn't say much,' said Effie. 'Well nothing more than they
already knew.'

'That's the best way,' said Oscar looking over at the table where
the instructors were sitting. 'That leaves you and me, Milo. What do
you reckon?'

I shrugged. 'I don't know,' I said. 'They all look so friendly.'

86

'I know, but that's what I told you. They're all nice, nice, trying to be ur friend, then bam! You get what she did last night. We've got to –'

'Okay, guys.' Lois was standing by the side of the noticeboard. 'e've made a few changes, as you can see.'

'Yeah,' Oscar mumbled, then glanced at Matty.

'But the biggest change of all is that it's too hot to be out in the 1 today so we think the best thing to do is visit the mine. But don't rry, we'll look at doing some of the other things tomorrow as the ather forecast says it should be cooler.'

'But that means we've got to climb up that slag heap,' said Oscar.

'You'll be fine, Oscar,' Matty shouted out from his table. 'Just ke sure you fill your water bottle. In fact,' he said standing up, at applies to everyone. Fill up with water. If you've got two ttles, take both of them as we won't have another chance until we me out of the mine. But the good news is you've all got a miner's ch ... Pasties.'

'Pasties?' moaned Oscar. 'I hate pasties. Why can't we just stay in : dorms? It's cool in there. We could watch another film. Milo wants He said he wanted to watch Spider-Man.'

Yay!

miled at the thought of Luke getting excited, but I'd not said that to car, and from the wry grin on Matty's face, I think he knew.

'So, ten minutes and we'll make a move,' he said.

Oscar took a deep breath like he was giving up, but all he was doing is getting enough air to speak again.

'But why?' he said, pointing at the slag heap. 'Look at it, it's hu
You say it's hot, well, that's about the hottest thing we can do.'

The instructors looked at each other.

'Maybe come and chat about it,' said Trey, 'as everyone else see
to be okay.'

'They're not okay, they just don't want to say,' said Oscar. 'I me
isn't there a chairlift or something?'

'Chairlift,' Trey laughed, like he thought that might calm Os
down. 'Where do you think we are? The Alps?'

'No,' said Oscar. 'It's not funny. Don't laugh at me.'

Matty walked towards us.

'Oscar,' he said calmly. 'No one's laughing at you.'

'Then what are you doing, then? It looks like laughing to me.' H
face had turned red, and it wasn't because of the heat.

'Oscar,' said Matty. 'Why don't we just go inside and try
calm down.'

'I will,' said Oscar. 'I will go inside. But on my own.'

He stood up, knocking the table with his leg as he stormed insi

Everyone looked at each other, not knowing what to say or do.

Lois walked towards the dorms.

I looked at Effie, who seemed as shocked as I felt. What h
happened to Oscar? One minute he had seemed calm, the next he
gone off like a firework. Was it because he had to climb a hill, or w
he just trying anything to get away from Matty?

We were all spread out like a caravan of camels in the heat, with o
rucksacks on our backs as we headed up the hill to the mine, none

s talking, just walking with our heads down. It was like the shock of
Oscar kicking off had made us all lose our voices. Except for Oscar
imself, who had miraculously recovered and was now walking
ehind Trey at the front.

I was on my own chatting to Luke because he was feeling left
ut.

> I'm sorry, Lukey. It's just harder to talk with Effie and
> Oscar around.
> *So you haven't forgotten me?*
> Of course not. Never will.
> *That's cool. So we're still friends.*
> Course. We're brothers.
> *And no one can tell us apart.*
> Tear us.
> *What?*
> It's 'tear us'.
> *Oh, but it could be 'tell us', too. Everyone thought we
> looked like twins.*
> Yeah. I smiled. It could be tell us, too.
> *So, will you tell me a story?*

tried to laugh. Luke always wanted a story, but it was so hot and the
ill so steep that it was hard to talk and climb at the same time.

> *Just a short one.*
> Okay. I stopped. You choose.

The one about the boy who flew too close to the sun.

Icarus?

Yeah, I like that one.

But it's a bit sad.

That's okay. It's not like I would ever do it.

I smiled. I know, Lukey, I know.

I couldn't tell him he kind of already had.

Icarus had fallen into the sea, and Luke was being quiet for once, whe I stopped for breath and a drink. Six of the group were behind me with Matty walking at the back, which explained why Oscar was a the front, like he was getting as far away from him as he could. Th good thing was Matty was far away from me too, so I didn't have t worry about talking to him either.

I looked back down at the camp, at the buildings and the tables, an the minibus parked in the dust. It seemed weird that we were all livin down there in the dorms when there was so much space all around.

'How's it going, Milo?' Sabula made me jump as she cam alongside me.

Great, thanks.

'Yeah, good, thanks.'

Sabula puffed. 'Not too hard for you?'

No, we just had a great story.

'No,' I said. 'Not too hard.'

'Well, that's good to know,' said Sabula. 'What's been your favourite part so far?'

Zip-wire. Zip-wire.

'Not sure.' I shrugged. 'But I guess the kayak.'

!!

'Yes.' Sabula smiled. 'You seemed to take to that ... although it did look like you were having second thoughts.'

That was me 😊

'Yes,' I said. 'Just a few.'

Sabula smiled. 'Well, at least you overcame them ... And that's good.'

I nodded, even though I wasn't sure 'overcame' was the right word. It made it sound like Luke was an obstacle, something that got in the way, but he was never that, not even a little bit.

Thanks 😊

'So what about everyone else? How are you getting along with them? I see you spend a lot of time with Effie and Oscar.'

She's asking a lot of questions.

I know.

Friend or enemy?

Not sure.

Sabula seemed really nice, but if Oscar was right, I wasn't sure I should talk much about myself or them, and certainly not about Luke.

'Okay,' I said. 'We were in the same group for Kayaking, and we've stuck together.'

'That's good,' she said. 'We're mixing the groups tomorrow, so you'll get to know the others more, but it's good you've become friends.'

'Yeah,' I said.

'You don't sound so sure.'

'No, I am,' I said, stopping. 'I was just trying to get my breath.'

'Yes.' Sabula stopped too. 'It's quite a climb, but from here you can see up towards the moors, over there ... And over that way,' she pointed out to sea, at what I thought were clouds on the horizon, 'you can see the Scilly Isles. That's twenty-eight miles.'

Cool.

'Cool,' I said.

Friend?

Still too early to tell.

92

I waited for Sabula to say something else, but as two of the group passed us, it was like she wanted to just be quiet and enjoy the view and for once I was happy with the silence as it meant I had fewer questions to worry about.

The wind blew and cooled me down for a second. Then I heard the roar of a plane.

I looked up.

Out the corner of my eye I sensed Sabula looking too.

'Do you ever wonder where they're going?' she asked softly. 'The planes. And who's on them.'

Yes! We do. We do that!

'Sometimes,' I said.

All the time! We used to sit on our hill and watch them.
You'd make up stories and tell me you'd take me to
Fran San Sico, and then Disneyland.
Fran San Sico. Ha!

Sabula said something else, but all I could think of was me and Luke sat up on our hill, outside our house, eating sweets while we watched the planes. And for a moment I wished I could sit there and be with him again.

But this is okay, Milo. Isn't this the same?

I shook my head slowly.

No, Lukey, this isn't the same. I think she's trying to get
me to talk about you.
And?
And I'm scared what she might do after that.

'Milo.' Sabula stood right in front of me, so close I could see my face reflected in her sunglasses. 'I asked you where you would go?'

'Don't know.' I shrugged. 'Anywhere, really. Just as long as I'm not on my own.'

'Same here,' she said. 'Who would you take with you?'

Me! Me! Me!
Shush. I think she's digging, Lukey.

'Mum and Dad,' I said.

'Who else?'

I shrugged. She was getting too close to Luke. I needed to say something to throw her off track.

Penguins?
Good one.

'Penguins,' I blurted.

Sabula looked at me, shocked. 'Penguins?'

'Yes,' I said. 'I'm writing a story about the Arctic, and I'm not sure I can have penguins in it, because they live in the Antarctic, don't they? I couldn't check because we don't have our phones.'

'I'm not sure.' Sabula was confused. 'But maybe I could ask one of the others.'

'Cool.' I turned and looked ahead. The others had reached the mine entrance and were taking their rucksacks off and laying them on the ground.

'I think we should get going,' I said.

'No, it's okay,' said Sabula. 'We can stay here if you like.'

'No,' I said, hitching my bag on my back. 'I really think we should.'

I started to walk on. Sabula walked beside me, saying Lois knew something about penguins, then commenting about how steep the hill was and how the sun was baking her head. But I didn't care about the climb, or the heat. I didn't even really care about penguins. All I cared about was Luke, and how Sabula had made me think of him so much that my chest was aching.

Fran San Sico.
Yeah.
Lost Angels. Ha . . . Disneyland!
One day, Luke. One day we will go.

I sniffed and wiped my nose on my arm. Sabula put her hand on my shoulder.

Maybe we should tell her, Milo . . . It might help.
No, Lukey, you don't understand. Can't you see it's what they want?

95

'Hey, you okay, Milo?' Sabula leaned in front of me.

'Yes.' I sniffed as I walked on, following the tracks. 'It's the dust,' I said. 'It's getting into my eyes.'

Good one!

I sniffed again, then took another step. I was so glad I was wearing sunglasses so Sabula couldn't see my tears.

CHAPTER 9

THE MINE

Sweat was dripping down my face by the time I reached the mine. There were a dozen tin huts like the ones we were staying in, except that they were joined together and became bigger the higher we got. The website said hundreds of men had worked here, but now all that was left of them were black-and-white pictures on the walls and some old pairs of boots.

Oscar came and stood beside me, like he'd been waiting for me to arrive.

'You okay?' he asked.

'Yeah,' I said. 'I think so.'

'You think so?' He turned me away from the rest of the group. 'What happened?' he whispered. 'I saw you talking to Sabula. What did you tell her?'

'Nothing,' I said. 'It was ...'

'It was what?'

'I don't know, just the things she got me thinking about.'

Oscar shook his head. 'Yeah, see,' he said. 'That's what they do.

First Effie, then me, then you. They make you think about stuff. But this place is quite cool, though. I reckon we could skive off for a bit. They'd never find us amongst all this machinery and dust.'

'Boys!'

We turned around. Matty was holding up two hi-vis jackets.

'You need to put these on,' he said. 'And there'll be hard hats when we go underground.'

Oscar and I put the jackets on. I spotted Effie talking to Kaya and Hannah from another group. For a moment I thought maybe she'd swapped out of ours, but then she smiled and started to walk towards me, and the guide started speaking.

'So,' she said. 'Welcome to Starlings Tin Mine. I'm Tasha, and I'll be your guide today. Don't worry about this heat too much.' She waved a piece of paper in front of her face. 'Believe me, it will be a lot cooler when we get down the mine. But first, I'll explain a few of the things that we have up here ...'

Effie came and stood beside me.

'You okay?' she whispered.

'Yeah,' I said. 'Just a bit hot.'

We both looked back at Tasha, because she was showing us one of the hard hats.

'So,' she said, 'we'll be handing these out. All you need to do is put them on and adjust the straps like this, with maybe two fingers' width gap between the chin and the strap. Not so loose it falls off, not so tight you can't breathe.'

Matty and Sabula handed the hats out. Bright yellow with a torch on top. The group chatted and laughed as we put them on.

98

I searched for the strap and saw Oscar doing the same.

'Mine's too tight,' he said.

'No surprise there, then,' said Effie. 'What with your big head.'

'Oi!' Oscar went to playfully elbow her.

'Just saying.' Effie grinned.

I smiled as I struggled with my strap. One minute Effie and Oscar acted like they didn't like each other, the next they were joking around.

'Come here,' said Effie. She stood in front of me and put her hands up to my chin to fiddle with the strap for a moment. 'There,' she said. 'How's that?'

'Yep, it's good.'

'Great,' said Oscar. 'So can you feel that?' I winced as Oscar rapped his knuckles on my hat. 'Can you?'

Yes.

'Yes,' I snapped as I stepped away.

'Ooh,' said Oscar. 'Doesn't say much, but he can get stroppy. What about you?'

'Don't even think about it,' said Effie, holding out her hand. 'Or I'll stuff your head under that crusher.'

'Hey!' Tasha clapped her hands. 'Listen up, everybody, this is important. We're going to get ready to go underground now; we're just waiting for the party ahead of us to clear.' She stopped talking as her walkie-talkie crackled in her hand. I tried to listen but all I could make out was the name Steve, and then a load of static. 'As I'll show you in the next cave, to save time, the miners would drill another shaft, and pull up the tin that way. Also, as you see from the other two tunnels, if the vein – this shiny line of black and grey in the rock – diverted off in different directions the miners would follow it by digging new tunnels. We've barricaded those tunnels off, for safety reasons, so we'll follow the lights down this one, and I'll show you the shaft I just mentioned, and the air vent holes that lead to the chimneys. So, this –'

'Can you feel that . . . ? Can you feel that?'

I spun round and saw Oscar rapping his knuckles on people's hats, then laughing.

'Oscar!' Trey said sternly. 'I'm not sure everyone is appreciating that.'

Oscar seemed to be frightened of Trey, because for once he didn't reply.

He better not do that to us again.

Luke, I said you had to be quiet.

But I've been quiet all morning. Can I talk in a bit?

Yeah, in a bit.

'What is he like?' said Effie, shaking her head at Oscar. 'One minute he's kicking off because he doesn't want to be here, the next he's like this – happy-angry, happy-angry. Moods up and down like a yoyo.'

'I know,' I said.

'It's even worse for you,' said Effie. 'At least I get away from him during the night. What does he –'

The crackle of static filled the air.

'Okay,' said Tasha. 'The group ahead have gone through, so we can go on down now. Just to warn you – and I know this is obvious – it can be awfully tight and dark down there. But don't worry: it's perfectly safe. Now, just turn on your lights.'

We all reached up and clicked our lights on.

'This is cool,' said Oscar. 'Let's go up here, at the front.'

Me and Effie followed, passing the others in the group, with Matty, Sabula and Lois stopping behind the guide. I thought for once Oscar was being enthusiastic, but from the way he grinned I could tell he wanted to be at the front to get away from Trey, who was at the back.

We headed down a metal stairwell into a reception area.

'This is where the miners clocked in,' said Tasha. 'They'd hand a card to the foreman, who'd write their names down over here with chalk on the blackboard. That way they would know which miners were working at any given time.'

I looked up at the board and saw the names of the miners. Thyssen and Reynolds went down at 2.20 p.m. Davies and Trescothick went down ten minutes after.

Tasha moved on and we all followed her out into a yard where buildings surrounded us. We walked across it in single file, our feet scuffing through the dust. It felt weird to be walking the same path as those men had, over a hundred years before. But we were going down the mine for a thirty-minute tour. They went down for ten hours, day after day.

Is it okay for me to talk now?

Sure.

No one's trying to find me?

No, not now. But what did you want to say?

101

I wondered where the miners ate.

Underground, I think.

And peed?

In buckets.

Eew!

AWARDS FOR HEROES

'So,' says Dom Fox, 'let's recap. One very hot day in the middle of August, twelve children and four instructors all set out to go down a tin mine. What could possibly go wrong?' He rubbed his hands together like he was expecting the audience to react, but the only sound was someone coughing. 'Carly?' Dom looked across the stage. 'You've got someone with you who can give us a little more information about what it was like that day.'

'Yes.'

The stage light instantly switches from Dom to Carly, who's talking to a woman with blonde hair and glasses. I glance at Oscar, wondering who it is. Oscar shrugs.

'Tasha Kowalski,' says Carly, 'you were the guide that day.'

'Yes.' Tasha laughs nervously. 'I was.'

Even if she was the only person in the room, I'd never have recognised her in her shiny silver dress.

'So, can you tell us if anything struck you that day?' Carly continued. 'Anything that made you think it would be any different to any other trip down the mine.'

'No.' Tasha squinted under the bright lights. 'Nothing at all. I mean, we run seven guided trips down the mine every day during summer. Perhaps six hundred over the whole year. This group was just like any other, full of excited children looking forward to the experience. Of course, like Dom said,' she nodded to Dom who was now drinking a bottle of water at the side of the stage, 'it was an extremely hot day, but that wasn't anything to cause concern. In fact, the ambient temperature of the mine is around eighteen degrees, irrespective of the temperature outside.'

'So pretty comfortable,' says Carly.

'It is now,' says Tasha, 'but of course it was a lot hotter when it was a working mine, what with the miners' body heat, furnaces, and—'

'Of course, of course,' Carly interrupts. 'But this day was just like any other.'

'Yes.' Tasha nods. 'Sorry,' she says. 'Getting carried away with tour facts.'

'Yes,' says Dom, as he walks back across the stage. 'And we haven't got any money to pay you for that.'

The audience laughs.

'So, normal day, Tasha?' Dom holds out one arm.

'Yes.' Tasha nods. 'Normal day, normal tour, and we were all set to go.'

'Wonderful,' says Dom, grinning in the direction of a TV camera. 'And I guess this is where the fun starts.'

'Fun?' says Carly. 'I really don't think you mean fun, Dom.'

'No, of course not,' he replies, realizing his mistake. 'But, Tasha Kowalski, everyone!'

Tasha smiles, then heads towards the side of the stage.

Oscar nudges my elbow.

'Fun,' he says with an annoyed look on his face. 'What's that idiot on about! It wasn't fun, Milo, was it?'

I shake my head and look back at the stage.

No, Oscar, I think to myself. *It wasn't fun at all.*

CHAPTER 10

GOING UNDERGROUND / *UH-OH!*

The sun seemed twice as bright, and twice as hot, as we followed Tasha along a dusty track that led between the buildings. When we were down at camp I'd thought the mine entrance would be huge, but as we approached it, it just looked like an old wooden door built into a mound.

On the front it said: DANGER. ONLY PROCEED WITH GUIDE.

Tasha turned round.

'Quick numbers check,' she said.

Lois walked back along the line, counting as she went.

'Sixteen,' she said, including Trey, Matty, Sabula and herself.

'Great.' Tasha smiled. 'So this is the entrance. Once we're inside, the tunnels will lead us around fifty metres underground. Of course there are tunnels and shafts that lead a lot deeper but this visit keeps us a little closer to the surface. So, are we ready?'

Everyone around me nodded as Tasha pushed the door open.

I peered over Oscar's shoulder. Ahead was a narrow tunnel with a string of light bulbs running along its length. Oscar edged forward and followed the guide in.

It's very dark.

Yeah . . .

And very narrow.

I felt a gentle nudge in my back.

'Milo,' said Effie. 'Are you going in?'

Thinking about it.

'Yeah,' I said. 'Course.'

I edged forward into the tunnel, the beam of my torch lighting up Oscar's back and the wood and rock around him.

'Mind your heads as you go,' the guide's voice echoed back along the tunnel. 'In order to save time, and timber for the support struts, the men carved the bare minimum amount of rock away to get through.'

I don't like it.

It's fine, the guide said it was safe.

I followed Oscar as he squeezed through a bit where the rock narrowed, then crouched where the ceiling bore down. It was like being in a tunnel at the park, only you couldn't see the daylight at the other end. Just rock and wood, rock and wood with only the lights above to guide us. I waited for Oscar to turn round and say something funny, but he seemed to be so interested that I could hear him asking the guide questions, like how far did the tunnel go? And did the men always have torches?

107

'It's great you're interested,' said Tasha. 'But I'll answer your questions when we are all together.'

Oscar's torch shone bright in my face as he looked back over his shoulder. I couldn't see his face, but I imagined his 'I was only asking' expression.

We kept walking until the tunnel began to widen and turned into a cavern about the size of a classroom, with lights hanging from the rock.

We stood in a circle around the guide.

This is better.
Yep.

'So,' Tasha said, checking our numbers. 'We've all made it through. It's quite a squeeze, isn't it? Just remember that the workers were a lot smaller then, and to limit the number of times they had to come through, they'd bring their lunches, often pasties, and stay down here all day.'

'Blimey,' said Oscar. 'I feel like if I ate a whole pasty down here, I'd be too bloated to get back out.'

The group's laughter echoed through the tunnel.

Tasha smiled. 'Anyway, those of you who noticed the pieces of metal in the walls, they were to hold the candles to light the way. And when they reached this point, the cavern, they'd all be here, at the edges, chipping away at the granite with their pickaxes, at little purple bits like this,' Tasha pointed at a purple line that shone like foil in our lights. 'And they'd chip, chip, chip away, until the rock broke free, then they'd load it into the trays. The trays were taken up to the surface, where the pieces would go through the process I showed you, to be turned into tin. Okay?'

The cave flashed with light as we nodded.

'Right,' said Tasha. 'Let's move on ... This way ...'

I waited for Oscar to follow her, but all I heard was his sigh as the others filed away.

'What's wrong?' I whispered.

'This ... It was interesting at first but now I'm getting a bit bored.'

Me too. Let's get out of here.

'Come on, you two, get a move on.' Matty was standing with Effie by the tunnel where the others had gone. 'I think we have to pass two more shafts, then we make our way back up to the surface.'

'Okay,' said Oscar, scuffing his feet.

Matty shook his head slowly.

'In your own time, Oscar.'

I went ahead and followed Effie, as Oscar walked behind me. Ten minutes before, he had been asking loads of questions. Now all he was doing was complaining.

'I didn't want to come anyway,' he said. 'Who's interested in pieces of tin? There are thousands of Coke tins in Tesco.'

'Well, yeah.' Matty chuckled. 'And wouldn't we have a great time if all we had to do was go on a fieldtrip to Tesco?'

'It'd be better than this!'

The light on Matty's hat flashed from side to side as he shook his head.

'Come on, Oscar,' he said. 'Even you have to admit this is pretty cool.'

'Mmm.' Then Oscar mumbled something that sounded like, 'Definitely cooler than you,' but I don't think Matty heard, because he walked on down the tunnel until we reached the next cave where Tasha had stopped once more.

'Okay,' she said, looking up. 'There's the shaft up to the surface that I told you about, but the main reason we've stopped here, is that we're going to show you what conditions were like when the miners didn't have lights above their heads, like we have today.'

The members of the group looked at each other.

'Yes,' Tasha said. 'We're going to turn out the lights.'

What?

'It'll just be for a minute.'

No, Milo! Don't let them turn out the lights.
We'll be okay. It's only for a minute.
No, Milo. No. Don't let them.

Luke's panic grew inside me.

Please, Lukey. Please, not now. Not here.
Especially here!

Tasha held her hand up towards a grey switch on the rock.

110

'If you all just turn your torches off.'

I heard the clicks of sixteen torches being switched off. The only one left was mine.

I backed away towards the wall.

Milo, please, tell them we hate the dark.

I took deep breaths and tried to calm myself down. Luke used to get panic attacks and now his panic had become mine. Deep breaths, that's what the doctor had told me to do. Take deep breaths. That usually worked if things got too much for me in the classroom or at home, but that was way different to being fifty metres underground in the dark.

'Milo, are you okay?' Effie whispered, by my side.

'No,' I said. 'The lights, we can't let them turn off the lights.'

'Not scared of the dark, are you?' Oscar was on my other side. 'Oh, you need to turn your torch off.'

'No,' I said, 'don't touch –'

Oscar must have reached up and switched off my torch because suddenly the cave plunged into darkness.

Milo!

I couldn't see anyone's face. Couldn't even see my hands when I held them up. But worst of all, I couldn't breathe. It was like someone had put a sack over my head.

Milo, let's get out of here.

One minute, Lukey, that's all it is. Sixty seconds.

That's too long!

Deep breaths. I took deep breaths but with each one I was scared I wouldn't find the next.

'Can't ... Can't ...' I stepped back and tried to steady myself against the cave wall.

'Is everything all right back there?' That was Matty's voice in the dark.

No!

I put my hands on my knees.

'It's Milo,' said Effie. 'I think you should turn the lights back on.'

'Okay.'

I heard a click. Then another.

What's happening?

I don't know.

Another click.

'Ah,' said Tasha. 'Not to worry, there is a back-up generator if it fails –'

Generator? Fail? Milo, you know I hate the dark.

I'm sorry, Lukey. I forgot.

My head started to spin, or maybe it was me spinning round looking for a way out.

'I forgot,' I said. 'I forgot.'

'Milo, are you okay?' That was Effie. 'What did you forget?'

'What's wrong with him?' That was Oscar, then other voices were swirling around me, but I recognised Sabula's right beside me.

'Milo, what did you forget?

'Lukey,' I said. 'I forgot how much he hates the dark.'

'Lukey?'

'Maybe we should get him out of here,' said Matty.

Yes. Yes! Get us out of here.

'I'll go check with the guide.'

No time. No time!

'No time,' I said.

'We'll take him,' said Oscar as I gulped air. 'Come on, Effie.'

I don't remember any other words, just my arms being lifted like I was a puppet in the dark.

'This way,' said Oscar. 'Back the way we came.' He pulled me forward by my left arm. Effie was behind holding my right hand.

'Oscar, Effie,' Matty's voice echoed in the dark. 'I said, wait.'

'No, keep going,' said Oscar. 'This is way more fun.'

Fun? It wasn't fun. I needed to get out, but Oscar was acting like we were comedy bank robbers on the run. I hit my elbows against the rock, my helmet banging it at the same time, as we squeezed through a narrow gap. I looked ahead, hoping I'd see a shaft of light, an exit sign, anything that might mean we were on the way back up. But all I saw was a long tunnel, lit only by the flashes from Oscar's torch.

'I think we should stop,' shouted Effie. 'This doesn't feel like it's going upwards.'

No, don't stop. Don't.

'Oscar! Milo!' Matty shouted again. We must have been half the size of him but twice as fast, because his shouts had been right behind us but were now turning to muffled yelps.

Oscar began to slow, like he was thinking of going back too.

No!

My hip grazed against the granite, then my shoulder as I pushed past Oscar.

'I need to get out! I need to get out.'

I rushed out into what must have been the first cave, but instead of lights leading the way back out, all I could see was three dark entrances.

That way.
This way?
No, that way.

I spun in a circle, not knowing which way to go, only that we had to go up.

'Milo, you need to calm down.' Effie was right in front of me.

No. Can't be calm. Can't wait.

I looked ahead for light, but there was just more rock, and more rock, and the further I ran the more it felt like it was closing in.

Can't see, can't see.
Can't breathe. Can't breathe.

'Go back,' I said. 'We've come the wrong way.'

Oscar was grinning at me like he thought this was all one big game.

'It's not funny,' I shouted, pushing him and Effie aside. 'Out the way! We need to ...'

I stopped. The rock was shaking beneath my feet, rumbling like thunder.

Oscar looked up. Silver dust rained down as the whole cave began to shake.

Get me out! Get me out!

We all turned round but granite lumps were now tumbling off the rock face, blocking the way we had come.

Oscar scrambled across the top of them.

'Come on!' he yelled. 'There's still space.'

The cave shook again. So much silver dust fell it was like we were stuck in a snowstorm.

CRACK!

I looked up as a lump of rock fell from the tunnel roof.

THUD!

It whacked against my hard hat, then tumbled down beside me.

My vision began to blur. I reached out for the tunnel walls, trying to steady myself.

'Effie?' I shouted. 'Oscar!'

A sharp pain shot through my head.

'Lukey?' I yelled. 'Anyone?'

More rocks, another sharp pain. My hand slid down the wall and I fell to the ground. I tried to push myself back up, but my legs had turned to jelly. Then blackness.

Black.

Black,

Black.

CHAPTER 11

STUCK! / *IT'S ALL MY FAULT*

Milo . . . Milo?
It's okay, Lukey. We're okay.

I crawled around in the dark, eyes stinging and throat thick with dust.

What happened? Are we stuck, Milo? Are we?
I'm scared.
One minute, Lukey.

I coughed. A stabbing pain shot through my head again. I put my hand
up to my cheek and felt sticky blood. I was alive, but it was so dark I
wasn't sure my eyes were open.

'Torch. My torch,' I said to myself as I scrambled around, confused,
but all I felt was the damp of the cave floor and the jagged edges of
small rocks.

Milo.

I know, Lukey, you're scared. So am I.

But where is everyone?

I don't know, but we'll find them. We will.

More damp, more dust – my hat must have been buried, or maybe the torch had been smashed by the rocks.

I really want to get out of here.

I know, I know.

I really do.

Don't cry, Lukey. You know I don't like it when you cry.

–

–

I heard someone groan.

'It hurts. My arm, it really hurts.'

'Effie,' I said, 'is that you?'

Torchlight flashed against the rock face, then right into my eyes.

'Yes.' Effie coughed as the light flashed left and right. 'What happened? And where's Oscar?'

'I don't know,' I said. 'I only just . . .'

'Oscar!' Effie shouted. 'Oscar, are you here?'

We waited for a reply, but all we could hear was Effie's voice echoing off the cave walls.

Please let's go. Please.

'Don't cry, Lukey. I can't do anything if you cry.'

'What's that?' said Effie.

'Nothing.'

Effie stumbled across the rocks towards me. 'Here,' she said, reaching down, 'put this back on.' She picked up my hat and rapped her knuckles on the glass of the torch. It flickered on then off. Effie rapped it again.

'There,' she said as the light lit up our faces.

I swayed back and forth and held out my hand, searching for Effie's shoulder to steady myself.

'You've got a cut,' she said.

'I know,' I said, touching the sticky blood with my fingertips.

Effie looked at it closely. 'I think it's stopped bleeding. But we need to find Oscar. He was right in front of us.'

I gently put my hat on and me and Effie followed the beams of light around the cave. There were lumps of rock all around us, some the size of our fists, others the size of our heads, and then one huge boulder, blocking the way we'd come in. The other way was a long pitch-black tunnel. I wondered if Oscar had escaped and run off down there in panic, but when I peered in all I could see was darkness and tiny pricks of light where my torch beam hit the granite. A cavern full of stars.

'Milo! Over here!' I spun round. Effie was in the middle of the cave, pointing at the bottom of the pile of rubble.

I walked slowly towards her. All the time her face was screwed up like she was too scared to look.

'It's Oscar,' she said.

I followed the line of her finger. A pair of white trainers was poking out of the rubble.

Oscar.

'Oscar!' I yelled as I ran forward only for Effie to yank me back by my coat.

'Wait,' she said.

'But Oscar,' I said. 'He's right there.'

'I know,' said Effie, urgently pointing at the rocks. 'But we can't just start digging.'

'But he's trapped,' I said. 'He might be . . . he might be . . .'

Dead? Is that what you were going to say?
No, Lukey. Stop. I can't think.

A small rock moved on the top of the mound.

I held my breath as it tumbled down the side and landed at my feet.

Run. Run!

I really wanted to run, but where could I go? And I couldn't just leave Oscar there, even if he was –

Oscar's trainer twitched in the dirt.

He's alive. He's alive!

'Oscar!' I shouted.

There was a muffled reply, then one more syllable that sounded like 'help'.

'Don't move, Oscar,' shouted Effie. 'Just don't move.' She held up her hand like doing that would magically stop more rocks tumbling down. Most of them were quite small, but there was a huge boulder teetering just over a metre above Oscar's feet. If he was lying in a straight line, the boulder was smack bang above his head.

Effie looked at me.

'Don't tell him,' she mouthed as she pointed at the boulder. 'If he knows, he'll freak out!'

Oscar called out again, this time clearer, like he'd somehow managed to find a gap to breathe between the rocks.

'Stay still, Oscar,' said Effie.

'What do you think I'm doing, you idiots? I'm stuck.'

If Oscar had been knocked out, it couldn't have caused much damage because he still sounded like his rude self.

Effie bent down and looked at the pile of rocks, like she was trying to work out the best way to move one without disturbing another.

> *Spider-Man would be able to lift them.*
> Yeah, I know.
> *And he'd get us out of this cave.*

'I know, Lukey,' I said, 'but Spider-Man isn't here.'

'Milo,' Effie looked up at me, 'are you okay? You're acting a bit strange.'

'Yeah,' I said, forgetting myself. 'I'm just a bit dazed.'

121

'Dazed?' shouted Oscar. 'What about me? I'm so stuck my legs are numb.'

His trainer twitched again. Another small rock tumbled down.

'No, Oscar,' Effie shouted. 'Don't move!'

Yikes!

Argh!

Spider-Man would have stopped that.

'Yeah, Spider-Man would've stopped that.'

Effie shook her head.

'Forget about Spider-Man,' she said. 'We need to do this fast.'

'Yeah.' I nodded. 'Sorry again.'

Effie stared at the stones. 'I'm thinking we start at the top,' she said. 'Lift them gently, try not to disturb the others. So that one,' she said, pointing, 'then that one, then that one, and we'll work our way down, then back to the top.'

I nodded and took a deep breath. Effie was being so calm while all I had was Luke panicking in my head.

'Get on with it,' demanded Oscar.

Effie leaned forward with both hands outstretched and picked up a piece of rock gently like she was holding a baby then handed it carefully to me. I placed it gently on the ground behind me, like I thought any vibration would shake the rubble and put Oscar in even more danger.

Effie picked up a smaller rock and handed it back to me. Then another. Now we'd started the rescue, it was like Oscar realised how scared we were because for the first time since I'd met him he kept quiet for at least thirty seconds.

I took another stone from Effie and turned round. My head kept spinning and my vision was dark at the edges, like the cave walls were closing in. I crouched down and put my hand on the ground to stop myself falling over.

'Milo.' Effie was right beside me. 'It's your head,' she said.

I took a deep breath, then another, trying to stop my head spinning and the feeling that I wanted to be sick.

'It's okay,' I said. 'I'll be okay.'

Spider-Man is never sick.

I chuckled.

'I'll be okay,' I said, looking back at the rocks. 'Spider-Man is never sick.'

'What is it with you and Spider-Man?' Effie smiled.

Everything.

'Nothing,' I said.

'Guys,' shouted Oscar, 'can you please stop talking about someone who doesn't even exist and get me out!'

For a second, I thought of trying to find a way through the rubble to get help, but it felt too dangerous to leave Oscar even for a second. Effie must have thought the same because she was already back at the foot of the pile, passing rocks to me. And each time I took one, I put it gently on the ground, like just one tiny vibration would bring the rest down.

We must have moved twenty rocks by the time we revealed Oscar's ankles, then another ten revealed his shins and knees. They had tiny cuts all over them, trickling blood and covered in dust. For a moment I wondered if they might be broken or worse, but Oscar hadn't said he was in pain, and he'd been able to move his feet, which I thought was a good sign.

Effie and I stepped forward and worked our way up to Oscar's waist. All the while, the huge boulder was balanced above his head. But we'd blocked it out of our minds.

'That's better,' said Oscar as we lifted some rocks from around his belly.

'Yeah,' Effie said. 'But Oscar, please stay still, you're not out yet.' She stopped and looked at the boulder. It was like Oscar was trapped under a mini Stonehenge. We couldn't even fit our arms around the rock, so there was no way we were going to be able to lift it.

I crouched down on the floor and looked up past Oscar's waist to his head. There was clear space between him and the remaining rocks, but one bend of his body, one twitch of his elbow could be the end. It was like he was a Jenga piece. We had to pull him out quickly before the rest came tumbling down.

'Oscar,' I said, putting my hand on his right ankle. 'Don't move a muscle.'

'Yeah,' said Effie, wrapping her hands around the left one. 'Don't even blink.'

'Wait,' said Oscar. 'Guys, this suddenly sounds a bit serious.'

'No, not serious,' said Effie, turning to me. 'You ready, Spidey?' she mouthed.

Ha.

I nodded.

　'On three.'

　'Yep.'

　'One . . . Two . . .'

　'Guys if this doesn't work, will you tell my mum and dad I lov—'

　'Three!'

CHAPTER 12

PANIC / *LOTS OF PANIC!*

'Is my hair okay?' Oscar was trying to be funny but I could see the fear in his eyes, after we'd pulled him out.

'Your hair is fine, Oscar,' said Effie. She sat down on a rock and put her head in her hands.

I looked around and for the first time I realised where I was. In a cave the size of a truck container, only I wasn't travelling on open roads, I was surrounded by rocks and rubble, with two others. And we were trapped underground.

What do we do now, Milo? What do we do?
I don't know.

I put my hands on my knees and tried to catch my breath.

Dad always says that adrenaline takes over when accidents happen. That's how he copes with all the blood and stuff when he turns up at a road-traffic accident in an ambulance.

That's how Spider-Man managed to lift the huge rock
that was on top of him when Vulture knocked all the
support bars down and trapped him under a building.
It's why Mum didn't feel any pain when she broke her
ankle playing hockey.
But what happens when the adrenaline runs out, Milo?
What happens when superheroes lose their –

'Help!' I shouted in panic. 'Help!'

'Help!' yelled Oscar.

Then Effie. 'Help!'

Help. Help. Help.

All of us, over and over, again and again, like our combined shouts
would somehow pierce the rubble. But even if they did, who would
hear them on the other side? Matty and Sabula had run after us; what if
the rocks had fallen on them? What if all the others were trapped too?

'Matty! Sabula! Are you there? Can you hear us?' Effie stood up.

'Please, Matty, please get us out.' That was Oscar. 'Wait . . .' He
reached into his pocket. 'I got my phone!'

Me and Effie stared at Oscar as he looked at the screen. 'No signal,'
he said. 'Not even emergency calls.'

No emergency calls! This is an emergency. This is an
emergency! Help! Help!

It was hard enough coping with my own panic without Luke doubling it inside me.

Oscar held his phone above his head. 'Still nothing.'

Help! Help! Help!

'Help! Help! Help!'

I bent down and put my hands on my knees again.

It's horrible. There's no way out.
I know. I know.

Deep breaths. Nice, deep breaths.

'Milo,' I felt Effie's hand on my back, 'are you okay?'

'No.' I shook my head as I gasped for breath.

Can't breathe. Can't breathe.

'No. Not really.'

'Then sit down,' said Effie.

'No, we have to get out of here.'

'Well, obviously,' said Oscar.

I heard Effie say something, but my head was now so fuzzy I couldn't make it out, all I could feel was her hand on my elbow as she lowered me onto the floor. I took another deep breath, then another. Meanwhile Oscar had gone back to the pile of rubble.

'Please, Matty!' he shouted. 'Sabula!'

No answer.

'It's useless,' he said. 'They can't hear us . . . they've . . . they've . . . they've gone. Unless . . . unless they are . . .'

Oscar could talk non-stop, but even he couldn't bring himself to say the *D*-word.

I leaned against the wall of the cave and hugged my knees. Effie put her hands on my shoulders.

'Stay there,' she said, pulling the hood over my head.

I tried to speak, but suddenly my jaw was set tight and I felt so cold it was like I had refrigerated bones.

So cold.

'I know, Lukey. I know.'

I wrapped my arms tight around my body and tried to hug us warm.

Effie knelt down beside me.

'Milo,' she said. 'Are you okay? Who are you talking to?'

Did I say Luke's name out loud? Did I? Did I? Can't breathe, can't breathe.

The side of my vision went blurry like the cave walls were vibrating and closing in.

'Milo!'

'Milo!'

I fell to the ground.

129

Black, all I could see was black, then nothing.

Nothing.

Nothing.

Nothing.

But then a picture.

A sunny day.

Me and Luke in the park, looking up at our kite – big red diamond, long orange tail, dancing across the sky. A dream of mine so clear it's like it plays on a cinema screen.

'Do you want to hold the string?'

'Yes, please.'

'Here you go. Put your fingers through the loops.'

'Like this?'

'Yeah, like that.'

'And I won't get pulled away?'

No, I laugh. *You won't get pulled away.*

The wind blows, makes our kite dive to the right, keeps blowing, further right.

'Save it, Luke, save it before it ditches into the ground.'

'How?'

'Pull your left hand down.'

'Like this.'

'Yeah, just like that. Oops, not so far.'

Our kite dances back up into the sky.

I look down at Luke. He's grinning back up at me, with gaps between his front teeth where some have fallen out.

'Am I gooder than you?'

I ruffle his hair.

'Yeah, you're gooder than me. Pull the left again. Pull your left hand . . . too late!'

Our kite crashes to the ground.

We both run over to it. The tail is okay, but part of the plastic frame is sticking out.

'Is it broken?'

'I'm not sure.'

'Let me see.' Dad stands between us, holding our kite in his hands. Me and Luke watch as he pulls at the plastic pole.

'Please don't be broken. Please don't be broken.'

Dad grimaces as he forces the pole into a hole.

'All done,' he says, handing it back to me.

And I'm so happy. In my dreams, I'm always happy.

Always happy, happy, happy.

Yeah, Luke, you're happy too.

CHAPTER 13

FALLING ROCKS /
THE DISNEY SHOP

Time on Oscar's phone: 1.25 p.m.

'Who do you think he was talking to?'

'Don't know.'

'At least he sounded happy.'

'Very happy. Must have been the bang on his head, sent him a bit weird. Not that he wasn't already weird.'

'Oscar!'

'Just saying.'

I could hear voices in the distance but still had the picture of me and Luke with the kite in my head. And I wanted to keep it there, to see Luke for ever.

'Happy, happy, happy ... What does that even mean?'

My eyes flickered open and I saw Oscar looking right at me. Then cold water on my lips and Effie's soft voice.

'Have a sip of water, Milo,' she said. 'And try not to move.'

I opened my eyes. Effie was right in front of me with Oscar kneeling by her side.

I took a sip of water and smiled.

'What happened?'

'Think it was the bang on your head,' said Oscar. 'Sent you a bit loopy. Talking to yourself and stuff.'

'Was I?' I said, thinking about how to hide Luke. 'Must have been a panic attack,' I said. 'I get those.'

'I think we were all panicking for a while,' said Effie. 'But you're okay now?'

I took another sip of water and let out a long breath.

'Yeah,' I said, looking around the cave walls. 'I think so.'

But we're still stuck.

I know, but you can't do that again.

I took another sip of water.

'Only drink it if you have to,' said Oscar.

'Oscar!'

'What? I'm only saying. I mean, we don't know how long we're going to be stuck down here.'

I stopped mid-sip.

'Sorry,' said Effie as she screwed the cap onto the bottle. 'He's right. But do you feel better now?'

'Yeah,' I said. 'Sorry.'

'It's okay.' She smiled as she sat down beside me.

'Have you heard anything?' I said. 'You know, from the others?'

Effie looked at the rubble.

'Do you think they're ... you know?'

'No.' Effie shook her head. 'We're not thinking that. We're hoping they made it out, and they've gone back up to the surface to get help,'

'Yeah,' said Oscar. 'That's what we hope.'

I looked at the pile of rubble. I didn't know how long I'd been out, but it had been long enough for both Oscar and Effie to stop shouting.

'How can you be so calm?' I asked.

Oscar shrugged. 'Not much else we can do,' he said. 'I mean, it's not like they can't get us out, is it? They must have plans for stuff like this. I'll check my phone again, might just have been a glitch.'

Yay!

'Yeah, try,' I said. 'Sometimes it comes back if you switch it off and on.'

Effie didn't look convinced.

'Not sure it will work, anyway,' she said. 'Otherwise, wouldn't the guides have used them instead of walkie-talkies?'

'Why are you so neg—' Oscar glanced at his phone. 'Argh, you're right,' he said. 'Still no signal ... But it doesn't matter,' he went on, still sounding optimistic. 'Like I said, they'll come and get us. They've got trained rescuers and stuff. I saw it on the news. Like those kids in Brazil stuck down a mine for eleven days.'

Eleven days!

'Eleven days!' I said, sitting up.

'Yeah,' said Oscar, 'but they were kilometres underground. We're only fifty metres, isn't that what the guide said?'

'Yes,' I nodded. 'But that's fifty metres of solid rock.'

'True,' said Oscar, glancing at Effie like I'd pierced his confidence bubble.

'So, what are we going to do?' I asked. 'How do we get out of here?' I looked at Oscar and Effie for an answer, but from the frightened looks on their faces, they didn't have one, only the same question as me. Our way back was blocked, and the only way ahead was a long dark tunnel.

Suddenly I wished I'd never spoken because Oscar's eyes were now full of panic.

'Stay still.' His light flashed as he paced around the cave. 'Stay still, yeah? We're supposed to stay still,'

'Yes,' said Effie calmly. 'And that means now, Oscar.'

She stood up like she thought Oscar and his temper were about to explode.

'I'm okay. I'm okay,' he said, still pacing. 'We have to stay still, that's what I did when I got lost at the shopping centre. I stayed still, waited outside Delish Donuts, because I knew Mum would end up there.'

Like me in the Disney shop.
Yeah. Just like that.

Effie laughed. 'Yeah, kind of like that, but I'm not going to lie, I think this is a bit more serious than getting lost outside Delish Donuts.'

Getting lost in the Disney shop was definitely serious.
Tell them.

'I dunno,' said Oscar. 'I was pretty scared. But I'm sure that's what we've got to do, just stay here.'

'My brother went to an assistant when he got lost in the Disney shop,' I said.

'What?'

Oscar turned and looked at Effie.

'My brother,' I said, looking up. 'When he got lost, he went to the assistant in the Disney shop. They put an announcement over the speakers. *Would Mr and Mrs Holmes come to the Meeting Point, where your son is waiting* ... They didn't say his name, just in case someone else turned up and claimed him.'

But they gave me a Mickey Mouse car.

'What are you going on about, Milo?' asked Oscar.

'They don't say names just in case a stranger turns up. But they gave him a Mickey Mouse car.'

Oscar laughed.

'You're brilliant,' he said. 'We're stuck underground and you're talking about Mickey Mouse.'

I shrugged.

He started it with Delish Donuts.
I know.

'Yeah, well,' said Oscar. 'Anyway, what do you think, Effie, stay still or go down there?'

'Stay still,' said Effie, looking down the dark hole. 'It's bad enough we're here, but who knows what will happen if we go down there.'

'Okay,' said Oscar, sitting down beside me. 'So, we stay here. But we need to plan. Might be ages before they get here.'

'Yes,' said Effie, 'we don't know how long it will be. First thing we need to do is think about what we're going to need.'

'Like water,' said Oscar.

'Yeah, and food and light. Like we don't need all our torches on at the same time.'

Don't we?

'But we should always have one on,' I said, sitting up straight. It was like Oscar and Effie were being positive and working out a plan. Unlike me.

'Only when we're doing something,' said Effie.

'But we can't sit in the dark,' I said.

'It'll be okay,' said Effie. 'With a bit of luck we'll get rescued before they all run out.'

'Right,' said Oscar, rubbing his hands. 'That's the light sorted, now what about food? Milo, what have you got?'

I started searching my coat pocket and felt a wrinkled sweet wrapper.

'I've got half a packet of wine gums.'

'Is that all?' said Oscar.

'No,' I said, reaching down for my rucksack. 'I've got the pasty they gave us.' I said, holding it up.

'Gross,' said Oscar. 'You've bitten a huge chunk out of it.'

'Yeah, sorry,' I said. 'But wait.' I dug deeper into my rucksack. 'My mum packed these.'

'Jelly Tots?' Oscar laughed. 'You still eat those?'

'Yeah,' I said, defensively, as they were Luke's favourite. 'What's wrong with that?'

'Dunno,' said Oscar. 'Just feels like kids' sweets.'

So?

'Well, if you don't want them.'

'No. No,' said Oscar. 'I didn't say that. What have you got, Effie?'

Effie searched through her rucksack, taking out items one by one.

'Half a packet of crisps, a *whole* pasty and a can of Coke. And what about you?'

Oscar shrugged.

'Nothing,' he said.

'What?'

'Nothing,' said Oscar. 'I did have some chocolate, but I ate it in case it melted, and I had my pasty as soon as they gave them to us.'

'What?' asked Effie. 'You said you didn't like them!'

'So what?' said Oscar stroppily. 'Doesn't mean I wouldn't eat one. Besides, how was I supposed to know we'd end up getting stuck in a—'

We all spun round, just in time to see a rock tumble down the pile and roll onto the cave floor.

I wondered if someone had moved it from the other side. We all looked at each other like we were thinking of shouting but were too scared to move even our tongues.

Another piece of rock tumbled down.

'Matty!' Oscar shouted. 'Sabula! Are you there? They must be . . . I mean, they've got to be.' Oscar's voice cracked with panic.

He stepped forward, started to climb up the rubble.

'No, Oscar,' I said, pulling him back. 'We can't do that.'

'But we've got to,' he said. 'They're right there.'

'No,' I said, looking up at the ceiling. 'I don't think they are. I think it's the rock cracking.'

Oscar had been so calm but suddenly it was like he had double panic.

'Help!' he shouted again. 'Matty, Sabula!'

All we wanted was to hear a voice, one little sound, from Matty or Sabula, Trey or Lois, anybody, just so we knew they were there. But there was nothing.

I heard another crack and looked up. Shards of rock started to fall and the ground rumbled beneath my feet.

'Oscar!' I shouted. 'Effie, we need to get out of here.'

I backed away towards the dark tunnel as the whole cave began to shake.

Effie ran towards me, but Oscar was still shouting.

'Oscar!' we both yelled at the same time.

Oscar stared at the rubble. He stayed still. Like his feet were set in cement.

I ran towards him and pulled him back by his shoulder.

'Oscar!' I shouted. 'We have to go.'

He turned and I pushed him in front of me, as pieces of rock fell like black rain around us, bouncing off the floor, pinging off my hat.

'This way,' shouted Effie, holding out her arm.

I pushed Oscar down the tunnel, his light flashing at weird angles as he stumbled and fell against the walls. I followed him, my feet and hands searching for ground and walls in the dark, but all I found were false steps and sharp edges as Effie followed close behind me.

The tunnel began to shake as the rocks fell behind us. We kept running with the tunnel spinning, our lights shining, not knowing if we were going up or down. All I knew was that I had to keep following Oscar as Effie shouted, pushing me in my back in panic. I kept running, kept pushing, kept falling, kept getting back up, over and over again, like I was trapped in the world's most scary computer game, searching for a secret tunnel where I could enter a password and find my way out ...

AWARDS FOR HEROES

The arena lights up blue and white as fire, ambulance and police lights flash on the screen. Dom Fox is talking as dramatic music plays. Oscar always wanted to be in a film, but I'm not sure even he liked it turning out this real.

'So, at this point, we know there has been a disaster,' says Dom. 'Here's how Dannielle Forstrup from SW News reported it at the time.'

The picture changes to a reporter talking into a microphone, with ambulance and fire-engine lights flashing behind her.

'The first reports are that a group went down into the mine, here at Swallow Heights, at 1 p.m. A party of seventeen went down, consisting of twelve children, four instructors and a tour guide. At 1.15 p.m. the staff on the surface heard what they thought was thunder until the ground began to shake beneath them. It's believed that part of the Dayman mine has collapsed. As yet we don't know the extent of that collapse, but we do know that eight children and three adults have made it back to the surface.'

The picture split in half to reveal a newsreader in the studio.

'So, just to clarify, Dannielle, that means that two adults and three children have yet to emerge?'

'Indeed.' Dannielle nodded. 'And as you can see behind me, in fact, all around me, a huge rescue effort is now taking place, with emergency vehicles from Devon and Cornwall, fire and police, as well as a team of cave rescuers. The camera pans out. Behind the reporter there are three fire engines and four ambulances, all with flashing lights against the buildings and the dust.

'And do we know the names and the condition of the people still down there?'

'Not at the moment. As always with these types of incidents, the emergency services are keeping very tight-lipped about the situation, quite understandably when family and loved ones of those who are down there are still to be informed. But we will keep you up to date as this very serious and dramatic situation unfolds.'

The camera pans away and switches to an overhead view that looks like it was filmed by a drone – the tops of the vehicles and the metal framework of the mine.

'Very serious indeed,' says Dom. 'Earlier we saw Doreen talking about her granddaughter, Effie. Now we're going to hear a little about Milo from his parents, and their thoughts about what was happening that day.'

The music stops and the picture changes to one of Mum and Dad, sitting in our living room at home.

Mum squeezes my hand.

'When did they do this?' I whisper.

'A couple of weeks ago,' says Mum. 'You were at school. Don't worry.' She smiles. 'We don't say anything embarrassing.'

I sit back in my chair as the camera zooms in on Dad.

'Disbelief,' he says. 'Total disbelief. I'd only dropped Milo off the day before. We just thought he must be having a good time. He needed a good time. It had been a hard few months for us all, but especially for Milo.'

The camera switches to Mum.

'Yes,' she says. 'Very hard. But he was doing well, you know. Just quiet, very quiet.'

I rest my head back on my seat as the view pans to the picture on the wall above the sofa.

I close my eyes.

I don't need to see the picture.

Please, why are you showing that picture? Me and Luke in mid-air as we star-jump off our garden wall – my mouth open wide laughing, his face beaming bright as the sun.

'I'm Spidey,' he'd just shouted. 'Shooting my webs.'

'I don't think Spidey does star jumps.'

'Oh, does it matter?'

'No.'

'So we just jump?'

'Yes, we just jump.'

'Ha!'

'Ha!'

'He lost his brother . . .' Dad's voice again.

I screw up my eyes tighter, trying to block his words out.

No, he hasn't lost his brother. He'll never lose his
brother. His brother will be here long after we take that
picture down. He's here, aren't you, Lukey? Always
here. Always, Always. Always.

I feel a hand on top of mine, too smooth for Dad's, too small for Mum's.

I open my eyes. Oscar's face is centimetres from mine.

'I'm sorry, Milo,' he says. 'I really am.'

I swallow hard. 'It's okay,' I say. 'We're good.'

CHAPTER 14

HOPE / *WHEN PEOPLE GET TOO CLOSE*

Time on Oscar's phone: 8.05 p.m.

Drip.

Drip.

Drip.

Drip.

We were aching.

Drip.

We had fallen against rocks.

And we had splashed through water.

And now we were so tired and cold from the wet that no matter how much we hugged ourselves, we couldn't get warm.

Why did the chicken stop eating—

No, Luke, not now.

Aw, go on, you love my jokes.

Okay, why did the chicken stop eating?

Because it was already stuffed.

They're getting worse.

I know.

Drip.

  Drip.

  Drip.

Oscar had said he had no signal, but for some reason he was still looking at his phone. 'What ... What ... What do we do now?' He was shivering uncontrollably now.

'I don't know,' said Effie. She was huddled up beside me, her torchlight shining out into the dark. 'But maybe we should all turn our lights on,' she said. 'Just for a few seconds, so we can get a better idea of where we are.'

I reached up for my light, clicked it on as Oscar did the same.

'Yikes,' he said. 'That was lucky.'

We'd come to a stop on a ledge, about as wide as a school corridor but only ten metres long. And about five metres below us was a lake of water that stretched out until the light of our torches hit the dark shadows of the cave walls in the distance. Together we tracked the walls round; sometimes they stuck out, other times they disappeared into dark coves our torches couldn't light, before emerging again. There was no way out, except for a small hole around the same level as the ledge, but even if we could have climbed down, the rock looked too shiny and smooth to be able to climb up the other side.

'I don't know if this is good or bad,' said Effie, 'but at least we're still alive.'

'Well, that's something,' said Oscar, checking his phone.

'Still no signal?' asked Effie.

'Nope,' Oscar sighed and sat down, far back from the ledge.

'It's like we're playing escape rooms,' he said. 'Only there is no escape.'

We sat down together, me in the middle between Effie and Oscar, who was still looking at his phone.

'You're not playing *Dungeons and Dragons* again?' said Effie. 'How can you get a signal for that?'

'Don't need one,' said Oscar tapping the screen with his finger. 'Besides, that's not what I was doing.'

'Then what were you doing?'

'Nothing. Just pictures Tyler sent me of them skateboarding down the park.'

'Maybe we should start thinking about saving the battery,' said Effie. 'Just in case all our torches run out.'

'Yeah, well.' Oscar's screen went blank. 'That's exactly what I was doing.'

'Only after I said.'

'Still did it.'

I stared ahead, trying to keep myself calm, so I'd not imagine Luke panicking again.

They always argue.
Yep!

Not like you and me.
Well, we do sometimes.
But not when we're in trouble.
True.

We sat without talking as one by one we turned out our lights. Then all I could see was black and all I could hear was the *drip*, *drip*, *drip* and the sound of our breaths. We didn't need to talk, we didn't even need to look at each other. We all knew that if Matty and Sabula, or any of the others, had been alive on the other side, there were hundreds of tonnes of rock between us now.

Oscar's phone screen flashed back on, then I heard the tinny sound of music as he put his earphones in.

Effie sighed. I considered saying something, but I didn't want to start an argument about saving battery again. Then it occurred to me that Oscar always seemed to put his music on after he'd blown a fuse, like when his mum forced him to introduce himself, and when he'd fallen out with Matty. Maybe he used music to calm himself down, like I took deep breaths and chatted to Luke. Just because Oscar was playing music didn't mean he didn't care. He might have been tapping his knee with his hand to the beat, but that didn't mean he'd given up hope.

Hope. Hope. Hope!
Ha.
Mum always told us there was hope. Hope. Hope.
Hope. No matter how bad things were.

Yeah, she did.

When I was home in bed. When I was in the hospital. I heard her telling the doctors, or maybe it was them telling her, 'There's always hope.' And then they would go out of the room and talk so I couldn't hear. Did you know what they were saying?

No, Lukey, not really. But I'm sorry, Lukey.

Why?

Because I don't want to think about that now.

Because it's boring?

Because it upsets me.

Okay. Did you want to think about something that makes you laugh? Like the time you spilt your popcorn at the cinema? No, no ... how about the time you told me a story and it made me laugh so much that I weed myself in Dad's new car?

I chuckled.

Ha, see. I knew I could make you laugh.

Yeah, thanks.

No problem 😊

—

I know you said you didn't want to talk about it, but this bit is happy.

Go on, then.

Sometimes I used to think Mum, Dad and the doctors

were making plans to take me somewhere, like
Wembley to meet the England team. Or Disneyland.
Ha! It's always Disneyland.
No, it's always Spider-Man.
True.
I loved my Spidey-suit pyjamas and shooting webs –
Tsoot! Tsoot!
Ha-ha.
If I had my suit now, I would get us out of here!
Ha. Ha. You would. But at least we've got hope.
Yeah. Hope. Hope. Hope. Hope.

I looked across at Effie, then Oscar. I couldn't see their faces but I wondered what was going through their minds. They definitely didn't have Luke in there, chatting away. But they must have been thinking about people they loved, just like I was. I didn't know much about either of them, only that Effie had said her parents were dead and that's why she lived with her grandma. At first, I thought that was sad, but then if she loved her grandma as much as she did, maybe it wasn't. And I knew even less about Oscar, only that one minute he could be funny and the next he would kick off and be quite mean.

Effie moved beside me.

'Milo,' she whispered.

'Yeah.'

'What are you thinking about? I heard you chuckle a minute ago.'

'Did I?'

150

'Yeah. You do it a lot.'

'Oh, it was nothing,' I said, trying to cover my tracks. 'I was just thinking about hope. My brother said we should always have it. And my mum.'

'Yeah,' Effie sighed. 'Hope, that's nice. My nan would say the same, but then I know she'll be worried too once she knows I'm stuck down here. She always says if there was a worry competition, she would win it.'

'That's nice,' I said.

'What, that she worries?'

'No,' I said. 'That you're thinking about her and not you.'

'Yeah, well,' Effie sighed. 'That's because I know I'm alive and she doesn't. And that's worse. I mean, we are alive, aren't we? We didn't all die and wake up in hell.'

I knocked my knuckles on my head.

'Yep,' I said, 'I think we're alive.'

'You're funny,' said Effie.

'Am I?'

'Yeah, Oscar was right about something. You don't say much, but you make a lot of sense when you do.'

That's nice.

'Thanks.'

'And I'm okay. But from the way you've been looking at me, I've had a feeling you've wanted to talk to me after what I said last night.'

'Yeah,' I said. 'Was it that obvious?'

'About as obvious as the rock hitting you on the head. Is it okay now?'

'Yeah,' I said reaching up. 'It's just a bit sore.'

I waited for her to say more about her mum and dad. After all, she was the one who'd brought the subject up again. It was like she'd said enough but I wanted to be sure. And it felt easier to say it in the dark.

'You can talk about it,' I said. 'Your mum and dad. I mean, only if you want.'

'What?' said Effie. 'Are you an expert on death?'

No!

I winced.

'Sorry,' Effie said. 'Did I say the wrong thing?'

'No,' I said. 'It's just that word ... but I'm okay.'

But you're not really.
No.
I think we should switch the light on?
Can we switch the light on?

'Milo? I asked if you were really okay,' Effie whispered like she was concerned.

'I think we should turn a torch on,' I said.

'Me too!'

I jumped as Oscar got up beside me and turned on his torch.

'I'm dying to pee. Where are we supposed to go?'

Effie turned her light on too. Her hat was in her hands lighting her face like a ghost.

'So, where do you reckon?' said Oscar, squirming.

'I don't know.' Effie was talking to Oscar, but she was looking right at me like she was still worried about what she'd just said. Is that how people saw me, an expert on death? I wasn't that. I was an expert on life. Luke's life. In the year since he'd gone, I'd never put his name in the same sentence as the *D*-word. And I never would.

I turned my light on, so all Effie could see was that and not my face.

'Come on,' said Oscar. 'Decide. I'm bursting. And I don't know about you, but my pee and poo are like trains.'

'Like trains?' Effie asked.

'Yeah, you know, engine and carriage, you don't get one without the other tagging along.'

I laughed. Oscar could be up and down, but for once I was glad of one of his jokes.

'Oscar,' said Effie, 'I've never heard anyone say that.'

'Me neither.' Oscar shrugged. 'I just made it up. Anyway, I'm going over here.' He walked to the edge of the ledge. 'And you're in luck. I think this time, I can hold on to the other.'

'Gross,' said Effie.

Oscar laughed as he undid his zip.

'You might want to turn out the lights,' he said, 'or at least look the other way.'

Me and Effie turned out our lights.

'Doing it now,' said Oscar.

'Yeah, okay,' said Effie. 'I don't need a commentary.'

Oscar's laugh echoed around the cave, and I was glad it did, because after what Effie had said, I didn't know what to say any more. I didn't want to tell her about Luke. I hated telling anyone about him. As far as I was concerned, Luke wasn't gone. Mum and Dad said it was like I was shut off, in my own little world, and the bereavement person said that too. I leaned back against the cave wall and closed my eyes. She used to whisper to me, but I could hear her words loud and clear now.

'It's okay,' she used to say. 'It's okay that you think about your brother lots.'

I'd nod. She thought I was thinking about Luke; she didn't know he was right there in my head, but it felt like she was getting closer.

'It's okay to talk to ourselves, Milo,' she'd say. 'It's okay to have little conversations in our heads. It can help with our worries if we don't feel like we can tell another person. And it can help us if we are stuck when trying to make a decision.'

'Cool,' I said, pretending I had no idea what she was talking about.

'So tell me about Luke,' she said. 'The things you used to do, the things you used to talk about. It's okay to have memories, so maybe you have photographs you'd like to share with me.'

'Not really.'

'Perhaps chat to Mum and Dad, and we could use them next time? Perhaps print them off from their phones or laptops.'

'Maybe.'

'Maybe.' And then she looked at me for a long time, like looking at me and staying silent would make words pop from my brain and out of my mouth. Or maybe she knew Luke was right there inside.

'You know, Milo.' She leaned in closer, so close I could smell her perfume and mints on her breath. 'Milo, sometimes the hardest part of losing someone is –'

La-la-la. La-la-la. Can't hear.

I didn't want to listen. Luke didn't want to listen, which was why he was singing away in my head.

'The hardest thing is –'

La-la-la. La-la-la. Go away. Go away. Why did the chicken eat bread? Why did the chicken eat bread?
I don't know, why did the chicken eat bread?
Because it thought it was a toaster . . . toaster, rooster?
That's not even funny.
Ha-ha.
Ha-ha.
But at least she's gone now.
Yep.
No drawing pictures of me today.
Nope.
No writing poems about the things we did.

Nope. Because she'd already gone out of the door, down the path and into her car that was parked in the rain.

Are we going to wave to her . . .? I think we should
wave. Goodbye.
Goodbye.
Goodbye.

CHAPTER 15

TALKING ABOUT LUKE /
READING OUR BOOK

Time on Oscar's phone: 11.05 p.m.

'Why did the chicken stop eating?'

'I don't know,' said Effie. 'Why did the chicken stop eating?'

'Because it was already stuffed.'

'Argh,' Oscar groaned. 'Milo, your jokes are as funny as being sick on a boat.'

> *Bit mean.*
> But true.

We'd been sitting on the ledge for three hours, according to Oscar's phone, sometimes talking, sometimes just thinking, but every once in a while, Luke would jump into my head with another chicken joke. When he was alive, he used to wake me up with a new one every morning, like he'd been in his bed thinking them up overnight. Now

I feel bad because sometimes when he laughed, I would just smile without listening to what he said. I wish I'd listened now. I wished I'd listened to every joke and every laugh . . . but just sometimes I do wish I could turn him down a little bit, even if I can't seem to turn him off.

'How about I-Spy?' Oscar said, like he knew there was another chicken joke being hatched.

'Really,' said Effie. 'You want to do that again?'

Oscar laughed. 'I'll start. I spy with my little eye, something beginning with *c*.'

'Cave,' said Effie, rolling her eyes. 'I spy something beginning with *w*.'

'Water,' said Oscar looking at me and grinning. 'Come on, Milo,' he said. 'What else is there to do?'

I shook my head slowly. We'd done I-Spy ten times over. Water. Cave. Oscar's trainers. My shoes. Effie's braids. Oscar's phone, over and over again. The first time it was interesting, the second time it was funny, the fifth time it was funnier, but now this, the tenth time, it wasn't funny at all. But the good news was that, by nibbling, slowly, we'd made my half pasty last for ten minutes, except for Oscar who ate his share in seconds.

'Okay, then,' said Oscar brightly. 'What's the first thing you're going to do when we get out?'

'What?' said Effie. 'Have you suddenly swallowed some positivity pills?'

Oscar smiled. 'We're going to be okay,' he said. 'One hundred per cent . . . So come on, what's the first thing you're going to do? Apart from hug your nan, of course.'

158

'Have a shower,' said Effie. 'No, a bath. I'll stay in it for ages, never want to get out.'

'That's not very exciting.'

'You asked me what I wanted,' said Effie. 'And that's it.'

'Yeah, but I meant something more than that.'

'Go on, then,' said Effie. 'If you're so good at this, what would you do?'

'McDonald's.' Oscar grinned. 'I'd go straight to McDonald's with Tyler and my other friends, eat a triple cheeseburger, extra-large fries and extra-large Coke, McFlurry, donuts . . .'

'Pretty much the whole menu, then,' said Effie.

'Yep.' Oscar grinned. 'And then we'd go down the skatepark, or better still Inox Hill. It's a huge hill where all the posh people live and they come out and complain about us, saying we'll scratch the cars, or the music is too loud. And then we'd all go back to McDonald's again.'

Effie shook her head. 'I think I'll stick to having a bath,' she said.

'No, you should try it. Actually, actually,' Oscar's face lit up as he began to grow hyper, 'I reckon they should have all of that waiting for us when we get to the surface, serve it like a banquet – us three and our mums and dads . . . Well, your nan, Eff,' he said, realising his mistake. 'It'll be fun, even better with all the cameras on us.'

'Cameras,' said Effie. 'What cameras? We've only been down here eight hours.'

'I know, but who knows how long it could be? Might be hours, might be days. Either way, everyone will be so excited when we get out of here. Remember those kids that got lost on the moors? They were all over the news for ages. And this is way better than that.'

'Oh yeah,' said Effie. 'Way better.'

'It is,' said Oscar. 'I mean, we're three kids stuck down a mine. That doesn't happen every day. In fact, it might actually be better if we get stuck down here a few more days, just to make it even more dramatic, as long as we live, of course.'

'Of course,' said Effie, rolling her eyes.

'In fact,' said Oscar standing up, 'they might even make this into a film. We'll be on Netflix, Amazon ... Blimey, they might even let us play ourselves and we'll get to go to the Oscars award ceremony in Hollywood.'

'Of course,' Effie laughed. 'It has to be the Oscars.'

'Yeah.' Oscar grinned. 'Your part would be easy, Milo. You're so quiet, but I'd make sure the writers gave you a few more lines, to make you more interesting.'

'Thanks,' I said.

'No problem,' said Oscar. 'I mean, we can't all be the main star.'

Effie sighed. 'Oscar,' she said, 'have you ever thought you might be a bit insensitive?'

'What, me?'

'Yeah, I mean you say stuff about my nan and you don't even know her, and you've said stuff about Milo when you've only known him a few hours.'

'Ah.' Oscar waved his hand. 'You're too serious.'

'I'm not.'

'Okay, then,' he said. 'How about I shut up? Let's see what happens then.'

Effie and I looked at each other but couldn't think of anything to say.

Why did the chicken . . .
Nope!

'See?' said Oscar. 'You can't think of anything. Not one thing about what you want to do when we get out.'

We can. We can think of something.
But not now.
Please, Milo. It's horrible when it's quiet. Tell them more about me. I like it when you talk about me.
Okay, I will.

I got myself ready to speak, but I'd been quiet for so long I often forgot how to start.

It's easy, just do what Oscar did. Tell them what you'd like to do when you get out.
Okay. I will.

'I'd like to hug my brother,' I said.

Aww.

'Oh, he speaks!'
   'Oscar!' Effie scowled.

'What?' said Oscar. 'Just saying ... but go on, Milo, tell us more.'
I shrugged. 'Just that, really,' I said. 'Nothing much else to say.'
'Luke?' said Effie. 'How old is he?'

Yay! She remembered my name.

'Six,' I said. 'He's six. I'd hug him loads then we'd go to our bedroom and watch a Spider-Man movie.'

Yes!

'So, it's not just you who loves Spider-Man?' asked Oscar.
'Sorry?'
'Spider-Man. You kept going on for it to be shown the other night.'
'Oh yeah,' I said. 'Yeah, I love Spider-Man, but maybe not as much as him.'

Tell them I had Spidey pyjamas and used to shoot webs.

'He used to pretend to shoot webs,' I said.
Tsoooot! Tsooot!
'Aw,' said Effie, 'he sounds so cute.'

That's me!

'He was,' I said.

'Was?' asked Effie. 'That makes him sound like he's –'

Don't let her say it!

'Is!' I said jumping in. 'I meant is. Mum and Dad bought it for his birthday. He wore it all day, in fact he wore it all week. After school, and to bed. Mum said she practically had to peel it off him because it was beginning to stink.'

Effie laughed.

'That's a funny story,' she said. 'Reminds me of when I had my Tigger onesie and did the same.'

I waited for Oscar to jump in and say everything we were talking about was stupid. But it was like he wanted to hear more about Luke too.

'What else would you do?' he said. 'After watching Spider-Man.'

'Depends,' I said. 'If it was late, he'd have to go to bed, but if not, I'd read him a story. *The Boy, the Girl and the Lion*.'

'I love that book!' said Effie. 'It was our class read in Year Six. Mr Severs used to do the voice of the lion.'

That's my part!

'I heard him reading it last night,' said Oscar. 'I had to tell him to be quiet because he was reading it out loud.'

'Yeah,' I said. 'Sorry about that.'

'No worries,' said Oscar. 'Pity you've not got it with you now. We could do with some entertainment.'

I looked at him, wondering if he was setting me up so he could poke fun.

But we know it! We know it!

'I can remember it,' I said cautiously. 'I mean, I've read it so many times I know it off by heart.'

'Then do it!' Effie said, kneeling up.

I looked at my rucksack like the book was in there. I took it everywhere with me, but I'd figured I wouldn't need it in a mine. The first line was ready in my head, but I'd only read it to Luke. It didn't feel right to share it with anyone else.

'Go on,' said Oscar. 'It's not like we've got anything else to do.'

'Oscar!' Effie scowled. 'That's not the way to get someone to do what you want. Milo will only want to tell it if he knows we really want to hear it.'

'But he knows, it was me that asked.' Then he turned and looked at me. 'Tell you what,' he said. 'We've all got to do something, just to be fair.'

I sat back, hoping that Effie and Oscar would argue like normal and forget I was even there.

Spoilsport.
Sorry. But I think our stories are just for you and me.

'Go on, then,' said Effie. 'What are you thinking?'

'Okay,' said Oscar, fidgeting. 'Milo tells us the story, and I'll . . .'

164

'You'll what?'

'Sing,' said Oscar.

'You'll sing,' said Effie sarcastically.

'Yeah,' said Oscar. 'What's wrong with that? I'm in the school choir.'

'Really?' said Effie. 'You are in the school choir. Well, that'll be interesting.'

'Yeah, well, it will be,' said Oscar. 'You'll see. And you'd better be thinking of what you're going to do, while Milo is telling us the story.'

They both looked at me. They hadn't forgotten me after all.

Go on, Milo. Do it. Their lights will be out.

Okay.

Yes!

'Okay,' I said.

'Cool,' said Oscar, leaning back against the rock. 'This is going to be good.' I still wasn't sure he was being serious, but he was now sitting forward like he couldn't wait for me to start.

Effie and Oscar turned their torches off. In my head, I opened the book to the first page.

'Okay,' I said, clearing my throat. 'Once there was a boy, a girl and a lion, and this is the story of how they all came to meet, in the middle of the Amazon rainforest.'

Can we skip to the good part?

Luke!

Joking. Every bit is the good part.

I smiled to myself as it felt like Luke was right there beside me, snuggled under the duvet like we did at home. When I would whisper-read so we didn't wake up Mum and Dad. I imagined Luke holding the torch, eating cheese-and-onion crisps and breathing quietly into my ear.

This is nice.
I know.
It's very nice.

I smiled in the dark as I said the next line:

'They were sent to live with the Yanomami tribe, in a village deep in the heart of the Amazon rainforest ...'

I took a deep breath and continued. I'd not read to anyone other than Luke for a year. I'd hardly spoken to anyone either, and now here I was in a dark cave with Oscar and Effie listening as I read every word. Talking was easier with the lights out. When I couldn't see people's faces. When I wasn't wondering what they were thinking about me.

'That's Milo, he's not been the same since he lost his brother –'

'That's Milo, it's like he's shut away in a world of his own.'

That's Milo.

That's Milo.

But there's nothing wrong with being Milo. I knew I was shut in a world of my own. Only it wasn't a world of my own, it was mine and Luke's world, where we still read, laughed and played. And now I was sharing it with two people I'd only known for a couple of days, and it felt okay. More than okay.

'It's good,' said Oscar as I paused at the end of the first chapter. 'You didn't stumble like I do, even with the book in front of me.'

'Yeah,' said Effie, 'and I love how you do the voices.'

That's me.
It's both of us.

'Thanks,' I said.

'So go on,' said Oscar. 'Keep going.'

Can I be the lion? Please let me be the lion.
Okay.

I rested against the rock and turned the next page in my head.

'"Good evening," said the head of the tribe.

'"*Roooooaaaaar!*" said the lion. "Good evening. I'm so happy to meet the Yanomami tribe.*"*'

Oscar laughed. 'See,' he said, 'it's great when you do the lion's voice like that.'

Effie shook her head.

'What?' asked Oscar.

'You,' she said. 'You're the last person I'd think would sit and listen like this.'

Oscar shrugged. 'But it's great,' he said. 'Go on, Milo.'

My heart swelled.

He loves the lion too.

I know.

Maybe do it louder.

Okay.

'"*Rooooooaaaar!*" said the lion. "Am I right in thinking you are the head of the largest tribe in the forest?"'

'Brilliant!' Oscar clapped his hands.

'"Indeed, I am,"' I continued, trying not to laugh. '"I am the head, and these are my people. As you can see, we have fires burning. Would you like to join us for supper?"'

'"*Rooooaaarrr!*" said the lion.'

I waited for Oscar to laugh again, but now he was lying back against the rock, like he was settling in for the rest of the story. I kept going, telling them how the boy and the girl and the lion ate dinner and danced to music. Then I got to Luke's favourite part, singing a song about a lion sleeping in the jungle. I'd added it to our story when I'd heard it playing on the radio on the way to the beach in Mum and Dad's car. I kept on telling the story until my eyelids started to droop. I waited for Oscar to tell me to keep going, but all I heard was the sound of him and Effie breathing.

. . .

. . .

So quiet, like even Luke was sleeping.

I marked the place we'd reached in my head then looked down.

Oscar's phone had slipped out of his hand onto the rock. I picked it up. The screen was locked but I could see the time: 11.56 p.m. It was dark in the mine, and it would be dark outside. I shivered. The guide said the temperature didn't change much because of the rock and the earth, but suddenly I felt cold.

I looked up, wondering what was happening above us. I imagined Mum and Dad talking to the rescuers, trying to find out what was going on, just like they did with the doctors and nurses when Luke was in hospital. I didn't want them to be worried like they were then. I wished I could shout through the rock and tell them I was okay.

I'm okay.

I'm okay.

Effie smiled with her eyes still closed, like she was some place nice, in her dreams.

I hoped that she was. I hoped she was with her nan. I hoped she was somewhere safe. I wished we were all somewhere safe.

I slid Oscar's phone into his bag, then lay down next to him on the rock.

My rucksack was lumpy, but it was my only pillow.

I turned out my light and pulled my coat around me.

Think of good things, I told myself. *Think only of good things.*

Can I help?
Ha, I thought you were sleeping, but, yeah,
you can help.
Thanks.

169

CHAPTER 16

GOOD THINGS / *UP HERE*
WE CAN SEE THE WORLD

There's blue sky.

Blue sky?

Blue sky.

No clouds?

–

No birds?

No, but there's a plane, with vapour trails behind it.

And we can imagine we were on it.

Where shall we go, Luke? We can go anywhere.

Except down a mine.

Ha-ha, yeah, definitely not down a mine.

Okay, then, so we'll take our kite to the park with

Mum and Dad.

Really?

Or the beach down the road from Nan and Granddad's

*house. Or maybe we'll go to London again and go
on the Eye.*

But I just said you can go anywhere in the whole world.

*Yep, and I said we'll go on the London Eye. It was too
hot, but I loved it.*

Tell me which bits you loved.

*All of it. The ice cream, the glass bubble, and I loved
looking out across London. I could see Buckingham
Palace and the Houses of Parliament. And the Shark.*

The Shard.

What?

That big shiny building was called the Shard.

How do you know? You weren't even looking.

I was tired.

You were clinging onto the sides.

I was looking after Mum!

Ha.

Do you think we could go there again? The Eye.

We can go anywhere, Luke.

Can we?

Of course. All we need to do is close our eyes and use
our imagination.

So we can go to America?

You always say America!

*Because that's where Mum said the doctors might be
able to save me.*

But this is a dream.

And?

You're not ill in my dreams.

Oh, cool. In that case we'll just stay here.

Really?

Yes. It's not about where you go, Milo. It's who you're with.

Ha. You got that from Mum.

Yeah. But she is right.

Yep, she always is.

I sighed, because suddenly just thinking about Mum made me miss her bad.

I rolled over onto my side.

Are we going to sleep now?

Yeah, we're going to sleep now.

Why did the—

You dare!

CHAPTER 17

SHOULD WE STAY /
OR SHOULD WE GO

Time on Oscar's phone: 6.03 a.m.

It had been dark when I went to sleep but for some reason, it seemed darker when I woke up. Maybe it was the thought of the sun rising above the mine, like I'd seen on the first morning, or of what I'd be doing if I was at home: listening to Mum and Dad getting up, then me going down for breakfast. Or maybe it was just that my stomach was rumbling and we were down to our last drops of water and last packet of Jelly Tots. I wanted some of both, but we couldn't risk drinking, or eating everything just in case help was longer arriving than we hoped. If help was coming at all.

I clicked my torch on as quietly as I could so as not to wake the others. Effie was curled up tight like a cat beside me, Oscar was on his back, his mouth slightly open, almost smiling. We were stuck fifty metres underground, but they both looked so peaceful in their sleep. I imagined jolting them awake by shouting that I could hear rescuers coming. Which way would they come – through the tunnel we had stumbled through? Along the hole we couldn't reach? Or from the ceiling? I shone my torch in all those directions, but all I saw was rock and a hole full of darkness. My happy thoughts of being with Luke were a long way from this. I missed him stacks already; I never thought it was impossible to miss him more.

Not up yet?

I waited for Luke to reply, but even in my head he didn't wake up until seven a.m.

I heard a shuffling sound and turned round. Effie smiled as she crawled beside me.

'You okay?' she whispered.

'Yeah,' I said. 'Can't sleep much.'

'Me neither,' she replied. 'I thought I'd found a flat area, but the rocks still stuck in my back. Doesn't seem to bother him though.'

'Yeah. He seems to be able to sleep anywhere.'

We both glanced at Oscar whose mouth was now open so wide it could catch flies. I smiled. Effie looked at me for a long time. I looked back down at the water. I knew that look from friends at school, the concerned look from people who knew Luke, but didn't know how to talk about him to me.

'Milo,' Effie said, eventually. 'Do you mind if I ask you something?'

'Course,' I said, turning to her.

'What happened to him?'

'Who, Oscar?' I replied. 'I don't know, maybe his mum dropped him on his head.'

174

Effie chuckled. 'No,' she said. 'I think you know who I mean.'

I thought of keeping up the pretence, but from the look on Effie's face, I could tell she was more than halfway to piecing together the clues.

'Your brother,' she said softly. 'You don't just read stories for him, do you? You talk to him too.'

'Yeah.' I sighed. 'I do.'

'Is that because . . .' Effie paused. 'Is it because he's dead?'

I tried to speak, but hearing the *D*-word about Luke made my words stick in my throat.

I think you should tell her.

It's okay, you can. I don't mind.

The *D*-word had hit me so hard that it had jolted Luke awake.

I glanced at Oscar.

'I won't tell him.' Effie said. 'He knows something's up, but he just keeps telling me that he thinks you're weird.'

'I suppose I am, really.' I shrugged.

'No.' Effie smiled. 'Not weird . . . well, maybe just a bit.'

I waited for her to say something else, but she just looked at me like she was waiting for me to get my secret out.

Go on, Milo. I'll even go quiet so you can talk.

I took a deep breath.

'Last year,' I said. 'He died last year. A week before my birthday.'

'Aw, Milo, I'm so sorry.'

'It's okay,' I say. 'Well, it's not okay, it's just that I've never told anybody. I mean, kids at school know, but they never knew what to say anyway.'

I looked up and saw Effie's eyes shining in my torchlight.

'Didn't you talk to anyone. A best friend?' she asked.

'Yeah,' I sighed, 'Zac. But he didn't know what to say either. He just kept talking about football and cars and stuff, like it might take my mind off it. But all it did was make things worse. I just wanted Luke to come back, and one day he did.'

'What?' Effie opened her eyes wide. 'Like a ghost.'

'No,' I said. 'Not a ghost, just in my head. It's not the same as actually having him with me, actually seeing him, but it's the next best thing.'

Effie smiled.

I was scared that she'd think I was weird too, like Oscar, but just seeing her kind face made me want to continue.

'My counsellor said someone never really dies until all our memories of them are gone. But he's not a memory, he's actually there. So we chat all the time.'

'I heard you,' said Effie, 'in the night. Is that what you were doing yesterday . . . The kayak?'

'Yeah,' I chuckled. 'Luke was scared. We'd been in a dinghy at the beach with Dad, but we'd never been in a kayak. I knew he wouldn't want to, but I had to make us do it.'

'Well, at least you did it, not like me.'

'Yeah.' I smiled. 'I managed to convince Luke that we'd be safe, but sometimes he doesn't listen, and he panics, and that makes me panic, too.'

'Ah.' Effie lifted her head, like what I said was suddenly making sense. 'So that's why you got so scared when the lights went out ... It's not you that's afraid of the dark, it's Luke.'

'Yeah,' I said. 'But it's hard to tell sometimes. It gets complicated, like I don't know where I end and he begins ... I guess that's part of the reason my mum and dad sent me here. To get him out, but I don't want him to go.'

'Aw.' I felt the weight of Effie's head on my shoulder. 'I wouldn't either. I think it's sweet.'

Friend or enemy? I think I already know.
Friend.

Tears welled up in my eyes. Talking about Luke, and not to him, was the hardest thing, next to not having said goodbye. I hated not having said goodbye.

I stared down into the water once more.

'Do you want me to leave you alone?' asked Effie.

'No,' I said. 'But I'm just thinking ... for a bit.'

My memory of what was Luke's last night in hospital played over in my head.

Hiss. Hiss. Clunk.
Hiss. Hiss. Clunk.

177

Do we have to think about this bit? Do we?

Yeah, Lukey, we do.

Hiss. Hiss. Clunk

Hiss. Hiss. Clunk.

I sat by the side of Luke's bed. 'I'll read you a story,' I told him. 'They say you might be able to hear me.'

Hiss. Hiss. Clunk.

Hiss. Hiss. Clunk.

I'll start. Once there was a boy, a girl and a lion.

I wished for Luke to open his eyes and jump in with 'I love the lion', but he just lay there on his bed.

Hiss. Hiss. Clunk.

Hiss. Hiss. Clunk.

I read him the rest of the story, leaving gaps for him to fill, but he never did.

Hiss. Hiss. Clunk.

Hiss. Hiss. Clunk.

I told him I'd see him the next day, read the story again.

Hiss. Hiss. Clunk.

Hiss. Hiss. Clunk.

A tear trickled down the side of my nose. I sniffed and wiped it away with my sleeve.

'Milo.' Effie rubbed my arm again. 'I'm sorry,' she said. ' I didn't mean to upset you.'

'I never got to hug him goodbye,' I said, looking at her.

Effie wrapped her arm round my shoulder.

178

'It's okay,' she whispered. 'It's okay.'

But it's not really?
No. It's not—

'What's happening? Argh! No!'

Me and Effie jumped as Oscar stood beside us, pointing at the water.

'It's rising! Why didn't you wake me up!'

I turned away and wiped my tears on my sleeve.

'Come on,' said Oscar, picking up his bag. We need to get our things.'

Effie stood up.

'Oscar,' she said, 'you need to calm down. It's not rising that quickly. Where are you going to go anyway?'

'Through that hole!' Oscar pointed. 'We'll swim across.'

'No,' said Effie. 'We can't.'

'Why not?'

'Because we'll get rescued,' said Effie.'

'Yeah,' said Oscar. 'By a submarine!'

Oscar stared at the rock, like he was trying to plot hand and footholds to climb it.

'I'm going,' he said.

Effie looked at me.

'Milo, stop him!'

I sensed panic in her voice, but it seemed to be about more than Oscar leaving.

I pushed myself up.

'Effie,' I said. 'What's wrong?'

Effie took a deep breath. 'I can't swim!' she yelled.

'What?' Oscar turned round.

'I can't swim,' said Effie, letting out her breath.

I pushed myself up. I wasn't sure which of them was right, but I did know we had to stay together. I shone my torch to the crack in the rock where the water had been coming through. Before it was a trickle, now it was like someone had turned on a tap. The cave was filling up, but I had to keep calm for Luke's sake, but also for Effie and Oscar too.

'You can't go, Oscar,' I said. 'We have to stay together.'

He and Effie looked at me.

'Why?' asked Oscar.

'Do I have to say it again?' she said, and then she did. 'I can't swim. That's why I never went kayaking yesterday.'

'Wow!' said Oscar, blowing out his cheeks. 'So that's why you got stroppy!'

'I wasn't stroppy,' said Effie.

'No?' said Oscar raising his eyebrows. 'Not just a bit?'

She was, just a bit.

'Okay,' sighed Effie. 'Maybe I was. But that's not important. I never learned. My nan never took me because she's scared of water too.'

Oscar dropped his bag on the ledge.

'Well,' Oscar said, 'that changes things.'

'Yeah, well,' said Effie. 'There you go.'

Oscar shrugged at me, like, what do we do now?

Yeah, what do we do now?
I don't know.
But we have to do something, don't we?
Do you have a plan?
I'm thinking.
Ooh, we've got a plan.

'How long have we been here?' I turned towards Oscar.

'In here ... this cavern,' he said looking at his phone. 'About seven hours.'

'And how much do we think it's risen?'

We all looked down at the water.

Loads.

'A metre?' I said.

'Yeah, I reckon that,' said Oscar.

'Okay, so that's a metre in seven hours, and we reckon it's another four metres to the ledge? So that's twenty-eight hours until it reaches us. That's plenty of time for them to rescue us, isn't it?'

'Yeah,' Oscar nodded like he knew Effie needed reassuring. 'Plenty. So we're staying?'

'Yeah,' I said. 'We're staying.'

Phew.

'Cool,' said Oscar. 'How about we celebrate with another one of your stories, Milo?'

Yay, story! And Jelly Tots.

'And Jelly Tots.'

   'Yeah,' Effie laughed. 'And Jelly Tots.'

AWARDS FOR HEROES

The arena audience is silent as on the screen a reporter stands outside the mine reading her notes under huge arc lights that illuminate the whole scene.

'It's now 2.05 a.m., more than twelve hours after the incident, but just this minute I have been told that relatives of the children and the two instructors still trapped have been informed, and I am now able to release their names. The children are: Milo Holmes from Bristol, Effie Thomas from Rhyl, North Wales and Oscar Hyatt-Davis from Brighton. They are eleven and twelve years old. And the adults are Matty Powell, aged thirty-four and Lois Anya, aged thirty-two, both from the Cornwall area. All their families are on their way to the scene.' The camera pans away, as the blue lights of the emergency vehicles fill the screen.

I look along the row at Oscar. I've seen my name in newspapers and heard it on TV, and it still sounds weird, but from the way Oscar smiles back at me, he doesn't find it weird at all. He's loving all the attention. I'm not. I don't want to be famous. All I wish is that Effie was here.

I look at the screen as it switches back to the Awards for Heroes logo.

'So,' says Dom Fox as he walks back onto the stage, 'I think, thanks to those pictures, that we have an amazing idea of exactly what the situation was, as it happened. With me now by video-link is Kate Nadir who was the co-ordinator of the rescue teams on that day.'

The picture changes to a woman.

'Kate, we know you are extremely busy. You had an incident in the area today.'

'Yes,' Kate says. 'But thankfully not quite as complicated as it was back in August.'

'Well, that's good news,' says Dom. 'So, Kate, I wonder if you could explain what you knew at that point, when those first survivors came up?'

'Well,' says Kate, 'we're going to show you some diagrams of the cave structure, and exactly where we thought the children were within it, but just to remind you, we were unaware of any injuries. And of course we had no idea if they were able to move, and if they had, which way they may have gone.'

The rest of the room goes dark as a white diagram appears on the screen. It's like the ant aquarium we had in the science room at school with a labyrinth of tiny lines along which the ants scurried. Only this wasn't a metre-long glass tank, it was a drawing showing caves and passages stretching for kilometres across the top of the screen, then dropping hundreds of metres below ground.

'So,' says Kate, 'this is the cave network. This point here is the surface: the museum, the mine entrance and then the main shaft that the children went down.' As she mentions each point a red dot flashes. 'And here,' she continues, 'here is the point where the cave collapsed, and then here . . . here is where the children were trapped.'

'And just remind us how far down that was,' says Dom.

'Well, the initial collapse was at around fifty metres, but due to issues the children encountered, and getting disorientated, like even the most experienced cavers do, they ended up around two hundred metres down. And just to put that in perspective, that's the height of the two London Eyes, or the length of two football pitches.'

There's a gasp from the audience, like they've only just realised how deep the mine was. And for the first time I realise how deep down we were too. And unlike the London Eye we were surrounded by rock, not air.

I stare at the screen, at the tiny stick drawings of me and Oscar and Effie. It didn't matter if you measured it in London Eyes or football pitches, either way it was a long, long way down.

My heart beats heavy in my chest. That's how small we were; that's how much rock could have fallen down and crushed us.

I glance at Oscar. He looks pained, like he did in the moments after the cave collapsed.

The screen changes to a picture of the rescue teams showing the type of equipment they used – lights, ropes, pulleys, stretchers and oxygen tanks. I shiver, but my hands are sweating as I twist in my seat.

Mum puts her hand on my arm.

'Milo,' she whispers, 'are you okay?'

I stare ahead. I don't want to look, but I have to look, just like you do when there's a scary film on TV.

'This rescue was difficult, for sure,' Kate continues, 'as some of these tunnels hadn't been navigated for years. We had plans, of course, but there was great concern for the children's safety, after more than twelve hours. Just one false move from the rescuers could lead to more collapses . . . and,' Kate took a deep breath, 'well, let's just say none of us wanted to think about that. But we had to give it our best shot. Myself and my colleagues set up a control room in the caving club HQ, bringing in laptops and radios as it became clear we had at least a forty-hour rescue on our hands.'

Forty hours. Is that how long we were down there? It felt much, much longer than that.

CHAPTER 18

OSCAR AND EFFIE /
LET'S GO TO DISNEYLAND

Time on Oscar's phone: 10.26 a.m.

When you tell someone your biggest secret, I think you're supposed to feel relieved. That a weight as heavy as an elephant has been lifted off your shoulders. 'A problem shared is a problem halved' – that's what I once heard Mum say to Dad when he had a worry at work. But after I told Effie about Luke, I didn't feel like a weight had been lifted or shared. Maybe that's because I never thought of Luke as being a problem, or maybe it was because I still wanted Luke all to myself.

Effie never mentioned Luke again in the three hours we were on the ledge. She just sat with Oscar whilst I told them the story about the boy stuck on an iceberg. Even though I'd not finished it, they loved the bits I told them. They even came up with ways it could end, like the iceberg would keep floating until it hit land, or the boy would get eaten by a bear (that was Oscar). I told them I'd think of something

187

spectacular and let them read it when we got out. Which made us all think about getting rescued again.

We decided that we should take turns to watch the water, selecting a rock that jutted out from the others as a marker. It had risen just over a metre since we first checked, which was around the rate Effie had worked out. So we still had twenty-four hours. All the while I was thinking that if Effie had worked things out about Luke, surely Oscar wouldn't be far behind. But for the moment he seemed to be more concerned that Effie couldn't swim.

'So how come you never learned?' he asked her. 'I mean, everyone learns to swim. At least they did at my school. Except for Josh Simmons, who always used to bring in a note from his mum.'

'I told you,' replied Effie. 'My nan never liked water, so she never took me, and we never had lessons at school.'

'But what about your . . . you know.'

'No, I don't know.'

'Well, are you going to make me say it?'

'My mum and dad?'

'Yeah, you know, before they . . .' Oscar's voice trailed away like he was scared to say the next word after the way Effie had reacted in the dorm. And I felt bad for her because if her house was anything like mine, the D-word was never said.

I think we should help her . . .
I was going to.
But don't say the D-word. Don't say—

188

'Oscar,' I said, 'I really don't think Effie wants to talk to you about her parents dying.'

Oops, you kind of said it!

Effie started laughing.

Me and Oscar looked at each other, shocked.

'You should see your faces,' said Effie. 'My mum and dad aren't dead.'

'But you told Matty,' said Oscar. 'You shouted it out.'

'Yes,' said Effie. 'But they aren't *dead* dead.'

I wish she'd stop saying that.

'I meant they're dead to me,' Effie continued. 'Like they're alive, but I never see them. And I never want to.'

'But that's still not good, though,' said Oscar. 'Right?'

Effie shrugged. 'I don't know,' she said. 'I don't really care.' She sat back on the ledge. I wasn't sure what to say, because her talking so much about not caring somehow made it sound like she did.

I flashed a look at Oscar. He shrugged like he was saying, *What are we supposed to do now?*

'God, you two,' said Effie. 'Are you just going to gawp at me? They left me, okay? Just left. I was eight, and they were arguing all the time, Mum blaming Dad, Dad blaming Mum, and then they both left and gave me to Nan.'

'So they split up,' said Oscar. 'That happens. Mine did too.'

'No,' said Effie, her voice strained. 'That's the point. They got back together, but they still left me with Nan, like it was me they blamed all along.'

Bit mean.

'Bit mean,' I said.

'Very mean!' said Oscar.

'It's off-this-planet mean,' I added.

'Thanks, guys,' said Effie. 'You're making me feel so much better.'

Oscar laughed. 'Sorry,' he said, 'but not ever wanting you back . . . !'

'Well,' said Effie, 'I don't care about them. My nan is great, and I'm way happier. She makes me laugh . . . She even took me to America.'

Ooh, Disneyland!
Not now, Luke.
Ask if she went to Disneyland!

I sat down beside Effie. She hadn't taken a weight of my shoulders with Luke, but suddenly I felt like it was easier to talk to her.

'How long has that been?' I asked.

No, not that. Disneyland.

'The last time I spoke to them was two years ago. But even then I just nodded at them, then went up to my room. Nan passes on messages that say they love me, but I don't believe them.'

'But do you love them?' asked Oscar.

'What?'

'It's a simple question,' Oscar said as he sat down on the other side of Effie. 'You said you don't care about them, but do you love them? It's not the same thing.'

'I don't know,' said Effie.

'That'll be a *yes*, then,' said Oscar.

'Okay, so maybe I do,' said Effie. 'But that's what makes it worse.'

I looked down into the water. Effie had said she loved her parents but didn't want to be with them. I couldn't imagine not wanting to be with the person I loved.

Me?

Of course.

I saw my reflection on the surface. It was just me, all on my own, when I would do anything to see Luke's cheeky grin by my side. Just for a few seconds. But then I'd want those seconds to turn to minutes, then hours, then days, then for ever.

Don't cry.

Milo, don't cry . . . I'll make you happy.

How?

Ask Effie about Disneyland.

Ha! You don't give up, do you?

Nope!

191

I looked up from the water. 'What was Disneyland like?' I asked.

Oscar laughed. 'Milo, you are amazing. I'm having a serious conversation for once, and you ask about Disneyland.'

'I know,' I said. 'Sorry, he . . . I mean, I just want to know.'

Effie smiled. 'It's okay,' she said. 'We didn't go.'

'But why do you keep going on about it?' asked Oscar.

'No reason,' I said. 'Just wondered.'

Oscar made a *hmm* sound. I looked back at the water, but I could sense him still looking at me. I needed to think of something else to say, before they started asking me questions.

'Do you think it's still going up?' Effie said, like she knew. 'The water?'

'About the same,' said Oscar. 'And it's only been fifteen minutes.'

I thought the danger of him asking questions was over but he was still looking at me. 'Milo,' he said. 'Is it your brother that wants to go to Disneyland?'

Uh-oh.

'Only, is he ill or something?'

'Oscar,' Effie said quietly, 'maybe not now.'

'I'm just asking,' said Oscar. 'Only you talk about him a lot, and I wondered if he was ill, like some of those kids that have collections so they can go to Disneyland.'

'Maybe we should eat,' said Effie, reaching for her bag.

I nodded with relief.

'Yeah,' I said. 'Maybe we should.'

'Okay, good idea,' said Oscar.

Effie pulled out her pasty. The foil was bashed and crumpled from knocking against the cave walls.

We all dipped our fingers in the mixture of meat, potatoes and broken pastry, taking just enough to make a mouthful. Even Oscar. Eating had thrown Oscar off the subject of Luke, but I knew it was only a matter of time before he asked again, so I told Luke to be quiet for a while, just so I didn't make any more mistakes.

After we'd finished, we checked the water level once more – Effie's calculations still seemed to be right. We were bound to be rescued by then, we told ourselves.

We turned out our lights to save the batteries and suddenly we were sat in the dark again.

'How about we take it in turn to tell stories?' said Effie. 'Milo already told us two, so it's your turn, Oscar.'

'Why me?'

'Because it was my idea.' Effie laughed. 'Go on, tell us one. And it can't be about your friends in Brighton in their cars.'

'Then I can't think of anything.'

'How about your family?' I said, trying to help him out.

'Something funny must have happened to you,' said Effie.

'Well, I could tell you about my sister.'

'You've got a sister?' said Effie.

'Yeah, her name's Lily.'

'Poor Lily,' said Effie.

'Poor me, more like.'

Effie laughed, but for once I wanted to listen to Oscar because he'd not said much about his family.

'How old is she?' I asked.

'Six,' said Oscar.

> *Oh, same as me* 😊
> I thought you were being quiet.
> *Sorry.*

'. . . She's okay, really,' Oscar continued. 'She makes me laugh.'

'Tell us a story about her, then,' said Effie. 'Like Milo.'

'Nah,' Oscar grunted like he was rolling over. 'My stories aren't as good as his.'

'Just try,' I said. 'I used to get nervous, but once you get started it's easier.'

'Yeah,' said Effie. 'We won't laugh, not unless we're supposed to.'

'Okay,' said Oscar. 'It's quite a short one about when my family went to the circus. We were sitting in our seats. They were temporary ones, you know, like the ones they put in the school hall for the end-of-term play. Anyway, we were sat our seats, watching circus stuff.'

'You can't just say that!' said Effie. 'Build it up, so it lasts longer, like Milo does.'

'Okay,' said Oscar. 'It was circus stuff, like trapeze artists and gymnasts. Oh, and yeah, there was a man who breathed fire like a dragon.'

> *That's cool.*

'Cool,' I said.

'So, all that happened in the first half,' said Oscar. 'But the important bit is what happened in the break when Dad went for ice cream and left me with Mum and Lily. She started being a real pain, getting up and down, wriggling in her seat. Fidgeting all the time.'

'Bit like you, then,' said Effie. 'Sorry, couldn't resist. How old was Lily then?'

For a moment I thought Effie had stopped Oscar in his tracks, but he was just working out how old Lily was.

'Four,' he said. 'I think . . . It wasn't last summer, but the one before. Or was it . . . anyway, she was fidgeting, and suddenly she fell between the gap in the seats, right between the slats. And she was hanging on by her fingertips, bawling at me and Mum to pull her back up, but we couldn't get a grip on her arms. All we could see was her red face looking up at us, like this . . . Well, you can't actually see me, but she was so scared.'

'I bet.' Effie's voice grew louder like she'd just sat up. 'So what happened next?'

'Well, Mum managed to grab one hand, and I ran down the steps and out through the exit to find Dad.'

Ooh, this is good.

'This is good, Oscar.'

'Thanks.' After being so cautious, Oscar was on a roll with his story. 'So, yeah, I found Dad in the ice cream queue, and we started to run back to Mum, but then we could hear a girl screaming really close to us. And we could see Lily's legs kicking because there was a clown underneath her, trying to catch her.'

'Noo!' Effie laughed.

Poor Lily.

'Brilliant,' I said.

'Yeah, it was,' said Oscar. 'I couldn't stop laughing. Imagine having your life saved by a clown.'

I was never sure about Oscar, but I liked him loads when he was like this, and for once his story sounded like it was true.

'What happened in the end?' asked Effie.

'The circus gave us free tickets and said we could take friends to go on another night. But we never went back, and now Lily hates clowns.'

'That's called something,' said Effie. 'When you're scared of clowns.'

Clownaphobia.

'Clownaphobia,' said Oscar.

Yes!

'No,' said Effie, 'but it is something like that. And it isn't very nice.'

'Yeah,' said Oscar. 'To be honest, I laughed at the time, but she does get frightened. Mum even has to check there aren't any in any films we watch. I feel sorry for her.'

196

'What?' said Effie, chuckling 'You? You feel sorry for someone? That must be a first.'

'What do you mean?' said Oscar, sounding hurt. 'Just because I mess around doesn't mean I don't have feelings.'

'Maybe,' said Effie. 'But I think I've got more feelings in my big toe.'

That wasn't very nice.

The cave went quiet. Oscar and Effie were arguing again, but for once Oscar didn't have a snappy retort. And it worried me that he didn't.

> *I don't like it when it's quiet.*
> Me neither.
> *Say something.*
> He might bite my head off.
> *But that was a great story. Ask if he's got any more.*

'Oscar,' I said cautiously. 'Are you okay?'

'Don't know,' he said. 'Might be.'

I imagined him pulling a sad face in the dark.

'Tell us another story,' I said. 'That was a good one.'

'What?' he said. 'So *she* can poke fun at me after?'

'Really, Oscar,' said Effie. 'Since when did you care about what I think?'

I waited for Oscar to come back with a sharp reply, but all I heard was a scuffing sound, like he was sliding away from us.

I heard a sniff.

Then another.

Someone's crying ... Milo, someone's crying.

I couldn't tell whether it was Oscar or Effie in the dark.

'Oscar,' said Effie. 'Is that you?'

'Leave me alone.'

'Aw, come on,' said Effie. 'I'm sorry. I didn't mean it, but we've said worse things than that.'

'Yeah!' cried Oscar. 'But we weren't stuck I-don't-know-how-far under the ground! I miss her. I miss Lily. I miss everyone, my mum, my dad, even my stepdad a bit. Even Mr McManus, my Maths teacher!'

Effie laughed.

'Then you really must be feeling bad, Oscar. Come here.'

Torchlight lit up the ledge. Oscar was sitting back against the cave wall with his knees pulled up to his chin. Effie followed the beam from her torch and crawled over to him.

'I'm okay,' said Oscar, wiping his tears on his arm.

'Yeah,' said Effie. 'It looks like it.' She sat down beside Oscar and put her arm around him.

'It's all right,' she said. 'It's okay to cry, but you're making me do it now.'

Oscar buried his head in his arms.

'What if I never seen Lily again?'

'You will,' said Effie.

198

'But you don't know that. Not for sure. She'll be lost without me, that's what Mum says whenever I go out.'

I didn't know what to do or say. We were stuck in a cave and for once Oscar wasn't thinking about himself. He was worried about his sister missing him and I knew exactly what that felt like. He'd been so strong up till then, and barely mentioned his parents, but it was like waves of panic washed over all of us and we were taking it in turns to crack.

'Want a hug?' asked Effie.

'Yeah. Wouldn't mind.'

I sensed Effie moving towards Oscar.

We should give him a hug, too.
I don't do hugs. Not since I never got to hug
you goodbye.
*Oh, yeah. Stone. Milo is made of stone ... Like a statue,
that's what someone in one of your classes said.*

I hated being made of stone. I hated watching Oscar and Effie hug and being on the outside.

Hug. Go on, Milo ... It's okay. We'll be okay.

I don't remember starting to crawl. All I remember is the rocks cutting into my knees, digging into my hands, as I made my way across the ledge.

And when I reached Effie and Oscar, I must have arrived so quietly that they didn't know I was there.

What do I do now? I thought. *What do I do?*

Easy, you just open your arms.

Effie looked up at me. I couldn't see her face, but I felt her hand on my wrist.

'You too, Milo,' she said, and she pulled me towards her. But I hadn't hugged anyone for so long I'd forgotten what to do.

I don't hug.
Imagine it's me.
No, that'll make me cry.
They don't need to know why.

I leaned forward, opened my arms and wrapped them around Oscar and Effie. I felt their hands on me; one on my neck, the other smoothing my back. Then the heat of their bodies against mine. The air was cold but I felt warm inside.

This is nice.
Yeah.
This is very nice.

'I never told them I loved them,' said Oscar. 'Not Lily, not Mum and Dad.'

We do. Every day.
Not everyone can.

'It's okay,' said Effie. 'You can tell them when we get out. We all can.'

'What?' said Oscar. 'You'll even forgive yours?'

'No,' said Effie. 'I won't go that far.'

Oscar sniffed again. 'Yeah,' he said, 'I know what you mean. Like I won't really miss Mr McManus. Don't know why I said that. He's gross.'

We all laughed and hugged each other again.

'But I can't wait to see Lily. And when I do, I'm going to tell her I love her. So then at least she knows.'

'In case you ever get stuck down a mine again,' said Effie.

'Yeah.' Oscar sighed. 'I don't think we'll do that in a hurry, do you?'

'No,' said Effie. 'But after all this crying, I think we deserve some more Jelly Tots.'

We let go of each other. Effie turned on her light, then searched through her rucksack. Oscar sat back against the cave wall. A minute before, we had all been crying, but now all that was left of our tears were the lines that cut through the dust on our faces.

We were crying, but we were laughing too, and that made me think that we'd be okay.

AWARDS FOR HEROES

'So,' Carly Wyatt walks onto the stage and stands next to Dom Fox, 'it's about this time, mid-afternoon on the second day, that some good news came from Cornwall, as two more survivors were brought to the surface. Lois Anya and Matty Henderson, two of the instructors from Swallow Heights.'

The screen fills with images from the surface of the mine. Lois and Matty lifting their hands up to their faces to protect their eyes from the camera flashes as they make their way through a crowd of people in the dark.

'As you can see,' Carly continues, 'Matty and Lois were immediately given blankets and taken to an incident tent, where they were made comfortable before going on to hospital. At the point they emerged, the pair had been underground for twenty-six hours and were suffering from shock and cold, but the good news was that apart from a few cuts and bruises, neither of them had serious injuries. But of course, it did mean the three children were still missing. Now over to Dom, who I believe is sat with Matty and Lois.'

I spin round and look three rows of seats back where Trey and the rest of the instructors are sitting. Dom is crouched on the stairs with a microphone in his hand. Next to him is a person holding a TV camera focused on Matty and Lois.

'So, Matty, Lois . . . You made it out!' Dom pauses as the audience begins to applaud.

Matty and Lois's images appear on the screen, smiling nervously, waiting for the noise to die down.

'Well,' says Dom, 'the audience is glad you made it out, but just take us back to that day for a moment. We've heard how you all entered the mine, but give us a sense of when you started to feel things were going wrong.'

'Well,' says Matty, 'to be honest, it all happened so quickly, but I'll do my best.'

'The group got separated, yes?'

'Yes.' Matty nods. 'There was a moment of confusion.'

I glance at Oscar, worried that Matty is going to put the blame on us for running off.

Oscar leans over. 'What's he even here for?' he whispers. 'He was only down there for a day!'

I chuckle. Even though we spent ages worried about Matty, Oscar still doesn't seem to like him.

'So yes, there was confusion,' Matty continues, 'but that can happen any time, and no one was at fault, especially when you consider that the lights went out.'

'But that was normal,' says Dom. 'Part of the underground experience?'

'Part of the experience?' Oscar protests, opening his eyes wide. 'I'd like to see him get stuck down there!'

I smile but I'm listening to Matty, still scared he might say something that will get us into trouble.

'Yes, of course,' he says. 'It was planned the lights would go out, for a minute at most. Unfortunately for myself –' Matty glances at Trey – 'for all of us, the lights didn't come back on. It was then that some of the children got detached from the group.'

I breathe a sigh of relief. Detached is okay.

'And then, of course, it happened,' Dom jumps in. 'The mine collapsed.'

Matty takes a deep breath. 'Well, yes,' he says.

'So tell us what it was like. Run us through the events.'

Matty swallows hard. Even from where I'm sat I can see tears shining in his eyes.

'Yeah,' he says. 'Yeah ... I'm sorry. It's just hard, you know?' He glances at Lois for help.

Lois leans across him and speaks into the microphone. 'Like Matty was saying, three children got detached from the group, and it all just happened so quickly. I remember hearing a cracking sound. It sounds obvious, I know, but just this huge cracking sound. One minute the children were in front of us, the next they'd disappeared behind a pile of rock and dust. There was no way through. Then seconds later, more rocks were falling behind us, and they blocked off both ways ...' She looked at Matty who had now leaned back in his chair. 'We were both panicking, initially for ourselves, but then it became more about wondering if everyone else was okay.'

'Indeed,' says Dom, grinning like he doesn't want the moment to be too serious. 'But the good news is that you did make it out, with the help of the amazing rescue team.'

'Yes.' Lois smiled.

Dom stands up. 'Lois Anya and Matty Henderson everyone! Not our child heroes, but definitely two very brave people. Back to you, Carly.'

The audience claps and cheers.

I turn back to the stage. On the screen, the camera has zoomed in on Matty, wiping tears from his eyes. He might only have been down there a day, like Oscar said. But it didn't matter how many hours it was, because I remember how much me, Oscar and Effie panicked in those first few moments. Trapped is trapped, like when someone sits on top of you for too long when you're playfighting.

Carly walks onto the stage.

'Okay,' she says. 'So with Matty and Lois safe, it's now the three children still down there – Effie, Milo and Oscar. We'll meet all three in a while, but for the moment, here are some interviews I did with their teachers, to give us an insight into their ability to cope with difficult situations.'

'Argh, no!' Oscar buries his head in his hands beside me. 'How embarrassing.'

I laugh. Oscar doesn't have to hide yet, because the first person that comes on the screen is my form tutor, Mrs Drake.

'Mrs Drake,' says the reporter. 'I understand Milo has been in your form for the past school year. Can you tell us a little about him and how he might have coped down the mine?'

'Certainly,' Mrs Drake says. 'Well, first of all, my thoughts go out to all the families of the children after this traumatic event. But I always had confidence that Milo would cope okay. He's a quiet boy, who likes to keep to himself. Maybe I should say he's thoughtful.'

'And what about his character, Mrs Drake?'

I glance at Oscar. He's right, this is embarrassing. It's like having your report read out in front of the whole school.

But most of all I can't think what more Mrs Drake can say because I'd been so quiet in class.

'Well,' she continued. 'Like I said, Milo is a thoughtful boy, but he also makes up stories of his own as he's a very talented writer with a wonderful imagination.'

'Very talented.' Oscar nods and smirks at the same time.

I smile.

Oscar goes to say something else but then his jaw drops.

'Argh! Bloody hell! No!' He's staring at the screen. 'It's only blimmin' Mr McManus!'

'Oscar, language!' his mum scolds him.

'I can't watch,' Oscar says, peering through his fingers.

On the screen is a man dressed in a black schoolmaster's gown, standing in front of an old mansion.

'You want to know about Oscar?' he says in a posh voice. 'Well, he's a very well-balanced lad. He's head of his year, and a very keen member of the debating society.'

'What?' I look at Oscar, wondering if his teacher is talking about the right boy.

The screen changes to a picture of boys in blazers standing in front of the building. The camera zooms in to the front row, where Oscar is sitting down with a black cap on his head and an uncomfortable-looking smile.

Mr McManus continues. 'I had every faith in Oscar as he'd been part of our Duke of Edinburgh team.'

'Duke of Edinburgh?' I mouth at Oscar.

'Don't ask.' Oscar shakes his head, then leans closer and says, 'It's not what you think, Milo. I was sent back after a day.'

'But you go to a posh school,' I say.

'Yeah,' says Oscar. 'And I hate it. Worse still, Mum's got a new job at a bank in Switzerland which means I might have to board there too.'

'But you said . . .'

'Shush, Milo,' says my mum.

I lean closer to Oscar.

'But you said she worked in a canteen!'

'I know.' Oscar shrugs. 'Because I wish she did. At least then I wouldn't have to go to that school.'

I sit back in my chair. In the mine, I wondered if some of the things Oscar said about his friends with cars, and skateboarding, were true, but I had no idea his life was as different as what I just saw. I want to ask him more about it, but the picture changes from his school to one of a woman wearing glasses, sitting behind a desk.

'Effie,' she says. 'Well, of course we were worried, but at the same time, we all had hope.'

Oscar sniggers as a picture of Effie with her hair in bunches comes up on the screen. But I don't feel like laughing. I don't feel like listening to her teacher, because seeing Effie on the screen makes me miss her loads.

CHAPTER 19

OSCAR / *FRIEND OR ENEMY* 😊

Time on Oscar's phone: 9.43 p.m.

We were now taking it in turns to sleep, which is why Effie was curled up beside me, while me and Oscar stayed awake, watching the water level, listening for the sound of a drill, a hammer, a shout, anything that might mean help was on its way. We'd tried to discuss with Effie how we were going to get her across the water if it came to it, but she didn't want to talk about it, especially as we had another eleven hours before it reached us.

'We'll do it between us, Milo,' Oscar mouthed, just in case she could hear us. 'You and me.'

I nodded and thought about how much Oscar now cared about Effie. I'd been so worried about him finding out about Luke that I'd not been on my own with him since we'd sat on our beds in the dorm talking. He seemed to realise that too.

'What did you think of me?' he asked. 'When we first met?'

I shrugged even though he couldn't see me. 'I don't know,' I said. 'Not much?'

'Oh, thanks!'

'No,' I said. 'I meant I didn't think about you much.'

Oscar laughed. 'Yeah,' he said. 'I knew what you meant. But what did you think? You don't have to say nice stuff. I mean, I know what I'm like.'

I took a deep breath. I wasn't sure what to say. All I knew was that Oscar seemed like a different person now, compared to the one who'd been asking me all the questions two days before. Back then he seemed confident, like he knew everything. Now he seemed no different to Effie and me. It was like being trapped made us all equal.

'Friend or enemy?' I said.

'What?'

'You asked me what I was thinking when we met, and that was it was, friend or enemy?'

'Like in war?' Oscar shuffled beside me.

'Sort of. But it's a game. Friend or enemy. I used to play it with my brother, like Stranger Danger, except it didn't have to be humans. It could be anything: hamsters, cats, dogs. Sometimes we didn't even have to say the words, we'd just look at each other like we had a secret code.'

'So you just go *friend or enemy*? And then decide? Just on what people say or do?'

'Yep, but it doesn't work on rabbits.'

'Rabbits?' Oscar laughed. 'Why didn't it work on them?'

'Long-haired ones,' I said. 'You can't see their eyes, so you can't tell what they're thinking. Luke got bitten once.'

Oscar laughed. I waited for him to say it was silly or weird, but all I could hear was the sound of his trainers scuffing on the rock as he knelt beside me.

'Go on, then,' he said. 'Tell me what you did with me. What things made you decide?'

I stared into the dark, wondering why he was asking. For once, Luke wasn't wittering away, but I imagined him saying, *go on, tell him, tell him*, but I didn't want to hurt Oscar's feelings.

'Does it matter what I thought?' I said. 'It's more important what I think now.'

'Yeah, it matters,' said Oscar. 'It's okay, I can take it. Like I told you, it's an act anyway.'

'Okay,' I said. 'But just as long as you know it's not what I think now.'

'Course.'

I took a deep breath. I couldn't work out what Oscar was doing. It was like he was a boxer holding his hands down, waiting for me to hit him.

Big ears. Big mouth. Stupid hair.

Ha, there you are.

Am I being mean?

Yeah. But he wants me to tell him something.

Just big ears, then.

'Come on, Milo,' said Oscar.

'Okay ...'

211

He looked rich. Nice clothes, two pairs of—
It's okay, I can do this on my own.
Okay.

'I thought you looked rich,' I said. 'You had nice clothes, two pairs of brand-new trainers and a nice watch. One of the best phones. Two, as it turns out. I couldn't work out why you were here when you had all that. Especially when you seemed so confident.'

'Yeah,' Oscar said. 'I get why you think that, but ...' I waited for him to finish his sentence but it just trailed off in the dark.

I heard a tap. His phone lit up between us.

I saw the time on the screen: 10.03 p.m. Then the weary look on Oscar's face.

'They're taking ages,' he said quietly.

'Yeah,' I said. 'Ages.'

The screen switched off, leaving us in the dark again.

I lay back against the rock. Oscar had asked me what I thought, but even though I'd not said everything Luke wanted me to, I was worried I'd said too much.

Oscar sighed, then his clothes and bag rustled beside me, as if he'd lain down using his bag for a pillow.

Not your fault. He did ask.
I know.

Tap.
Screen lit up.

10.04 p.m.

Screen turned off.

Tap.

Screen lit up.

10.05 p.m.

Screen turned off.

'Milo?'

Oscar's voice made me jump.

'Just cos I got everything, don't mean that's what I want.'

'How do you mean?'

'I don't know. Just saying. Like, your dad dropped you off here, right? Hugged you and stuff.'

'Yeah,' I said. 'He did. But what –'

'Just saying,' said Oscar. 'That's all.'

'But you had your mum.'

'Ha! Yeah.' Oscar chuckled. 'But I bet your mum wasn't here because she was working. My mum and dad didn't bring me here together because they can't stand being in the same car.'

'Sorry.'

'It's how it is,' said Oscar. 'It's just bad that Dad avoiding Mum means he also avoids me. Anyway, I don't want to talk about it any more.'

Tap.

Screen lit up.

10.06 p.m.

Screen went off.

I rested my head against the wall and listened to the trickle of the water. I shouldn't have said anything. I should have stayed quiet like always.

Screen lit up.

10.07 p.m.

Screen went off.

> *Hope he's okay.*
> Me too.

'Milo?'

'Yep.'

'Friend or enemy?'

> *That's our game!*
> I know.
> *But it's all right. You can answer.*

I smiled.

'Friend,' I said.

'Cool.'

Screen lit up.

10.08 p.m.

Screen went off.

'Good night, Milo.'

'Good night, Oscar.' I rested my head back against a rock. I thought Oscar had enough friends, but I was glad he wanted one more. And for the first time since Luke went, I realised I had space for another friend too.

I'm glad.

Me too.

But I'm still number one?

I took a deep breath and closed my eyes.

Yeah, Lukey, you're still number one.

CHAPTER 20

WAKE UP / *WAKE UP!*

Time on Oscar's phone: 1.34 a.m.

'Milo! Wake up!'

'W ... w ... w ... What? Where am ...?' I sat up, shaking myself awake.

Effie was standing in front of me, shining her torch in my face.

'The water, Milo,' she shouted. 'It's up to the ledge.'

I jumped up.

Yikes!

'Yikes!'

'Argh! No.' Oscar was standing near the edge with his hands on his head 'We must have all fallen asleep, Milo,' he said. 'The last I saw it was way down there.'

'But we had twenty-two hours,' I said.

'We did,' said Effie, 'but something must have happened.'

216

We all looked across to where the water had been coming in, but now the level was so high it was a swirling current, like someone had pulled the plug out of a bath. But the cave wasn't emptying, it was filling up.

'We've got to get out of here,' I said.

Oscar and I looked at Effie. She was frozen stiff, like the water was already up to her neck.

'You'll be okay,' I said. 'We'll look after you.'

'How?' said Effie. 'Nan always says I'm like her, that as soon as I'm in water, I sink like a stone.'

'But you won't,' said Oscar. 'We'll find a way.'

We all looked back across the cave. The water was now coming in so fast that that it had reached the tunnel and was lapping inside it.

We all looked back to where the water was coming in, then back to the only way out.

'It's filling up quicker than it's flowing out,' said Oscar. 'We've got to go now, or we'll drown.'

I bent down and picked up our rucksacks.

'These should float,' I said.

Effie stared at the water. I held my bag out in front of her.

'Effie,' I said. 'These should float. All we have to do is hang onto them.'

'But what if they don't?' said Effie.

'They will,' I said. 'I saw it on a survival programme.'

'But did they survive?'

'Course they did,' said Oscar, trying to sound upbeat. 'Besides,

217

it can only be twenty metres. By the time we push away, we'll be halfway there.'

'Yeah,' said Effie, 'halfway and then what? And we don't know where that tunnel leads. It could go anywhere. It could be a dead end!'

'Or it could be a way out,' said Oscar.

'I don't think so,' said Effie. 'Water only flows one way, and that's down.'

'But it's our only choice,' said Oscar, looking at his feet. The water was lapping over our ledge now and pooling around our ankles.

Effie took a deep breath, like she'd realised the truth.

'Okay,' she said. 'Just don't leave me behind.'

'Leave you behind?' He laughed. 'I'm pushing you through that hole first.' Oscar was being Oscar, trying to cheer us up, and it looked like it was working, because Effie set herself down on the ledge with her bag on her lap.

I sat down beside her.

Tell her we'll be okay.

The day before, Luke had been in my head panicking about not being able to swim. Now it was like he was back to help me.

'We'll be okay,' I said, looking at Effie.

'You think so?'

*Yep. All you do is close your eyes, close your mouth
and hope you don't sink.*

218

Good, but not quite right.

That's what I did.

I pushed myself to the edge.

'I'll go first,' I said. 'Oscar, you go at the back. That way Effie goes in the middle and holds on to both our bags.'

Good idea.

Thanks.

'Ready?' I said, turning to Oscar and Effie.

They both nodded.

I pushed myself off into the water.

'It's okay,' I said, even though the water was freezing.

I was trying to stay calm for Effie, but the cold of the water was taking my breath away. The good news was that my bag was floating.

I held it out behind me with my left hand, treading water.

'Come on,' I said. 'Just slide in. Hold on to the strap.'

Effie went to push off, then stopped.

'I can't ... I ca—'

'I'll do it with you, Eff.' Oscar sat beside her. 'On three?'

Effie nodded but the look on her face said she still wasn't sure.

'One, two, three.'

Effie reached out for my bag and slid into the water. Her chin dipped under the surface.

'Kick your legs,' I said. 'Just a little bit.'

'It's freezing. I'm try ... ing ... I can't ... I can't ...' Her words spluttered on the water. I pushed my bag closer to her. She reached out for a better grip but all she grabbed was air.

'Effie!' I shouted, swimming back to her. 'Stay calm, just ...' I held out my hand, but in a second she had disappeared.

Oscar jumped in.

'Where did she go? Milo, where did she go?'

'She was just here,' I shouted in panic as our torchlights flashed across the surface.

Oscar spun around as he trod water. 'The current is pulling us towards the tunnel, Milo,' he said. 'You go.'

'What about Effie?' I yelled.

'I'll find her!' Oscar took a deep breath, then dived under the water.

'Effie,' I said, under my breath. 'Where are you?' I tried to stay still, but the current was dragging me on. I looked down, but all I could see was the dull light of Oscar's torch as he swam in the dark.

My back hit the cave wall.

Oscar's light went out.

'No!' I shouted. 'No!'

Then I heard a splash and someone coughing, gasping for air.

'Milo!' Oscar shouted. 'I got her. Over here!'

I spun round in the water and saw Oscar by the tunnel entrance, with his arm under Effie's chin.

'She's okay,' he yelled above the noise of rushing water. 'But we've got to go, Milo. It's filling up too fast.'

I pushed my bag out in front of me. The current was now so strong I was with Oscar and Effie in what felt like a second.

'You okay?' I asked Effie as she clung to a rock like it was a life raft. 'Eff, are you okay?'

She nodded quickly. 'I just want to get out of here.'

'We will,' I said. 'We will.'

Oscar turned to me, hair dripping with water and a worried look on his face.

'It's about twenty metres,' he said, trying to get his breath. 'The tunnel, twenty metres.'

'Then what?'

'I don't know, that's as far as my torch let me see. Might go further, might drop away.'

'What do you want to do?' I asked.

'If it just drops away, isn't that even more dangerous?' said Effie.

'What's more dangerous than this?' said Oscar.

We all trod water, shivering with cold and nerves. It was like we were rats in a sewer maze, not knowing which way to go. All we knew was the cave would be full of water in minutes.

'You're right,' said Effie, trembling. 'We need to go.'

'Yeah,' me and Oscar said at the same time.

I reached out and pulled myself into the tunnel.

My hat rattled against the rock.

'We've got to crawl,' I shouted. 'There's not much space.'

I reached back for Effie, but she was already on her way in.

'Is Oscar there?' I asked.

'Just about,' replied Oscar.

I pushed my bag ahead of me, then crawled after it, stones

digging into my elbows and knees as my head knocked against the rocks above.

The further I went, the narrower the tunnel seemed to get.

I want to turn round.
I want to go back.
But we can't, Luke. Think of it like a waterslide.

'Keep going,' said Effie.

I reached out and pulled myself along, hoping that somewhere up ahead the tunnel would widen, but all I could see was rock facing rock with less than a metre's gap for my body. My heart filled with panic, but panic wasn't going to get me through. And if I stopped, Effie would have to stop, and then Oscar too.

I had to keep going, for myself and for them.

I reached out, pulled. Reached out, pulled. My fingers digging into the rock, my hat scraping the ceiling, the rock digging into my knees. And all the time, I could hear Effie and Oscar grunting behind me as they did the same.

I stuck my head down.

Keep going, Milo.
I'm trying. I'm trying.

The water started to rush around me.

Can't die. Don't want to die.
Reach out, pull. Reach out, pull. Reach out, pull.

I looked ahead.

'It's getting wider,' I shouted. 'Keep going.'

No reply from Effie or Oscar, just the roar of water.

One more reach and pull, one more . . .

'Aaargh!'

Falling.

Falling.

Reaching out for rocks.

Bashing and scraping my hands.

Falling.

Falling.

All the way down.

AWARDS FOR HEROES

'And so,' says Carly Wyatt, 'earlier, we heard from Kate Nadir, the rescue co-ordinator, who told us about the complexities and organisation of the rescue from the surface. Now we're going to hear from Seb Reid who was part of the volunteer rescue team. Here he is talking to Dannielle from SW News as the rescue attempt neared thirty-six hours.'

A man about the same age as my dad appears on the screen. He's wearing a yellow hat with a torch on top, just like the ones we wore.

'Seb,' says Dannielle. 'We're thirty-six hours into the rescue mission. Can you tell us firstly how it is progressing, and secondly, the conditions down there?'

Seb nods, then takes off his hat. Now there's a line on his forehead where the black dust from the mine ends and his white skin begins. 'Well,' he starts, blowing out his cheeks, 'the first thing to say is that it's going very slowly, but it really has to. As we're getting further into the mine, we're coming across fallen debris, and we're having to bring that out by hand because we just can't risk the effects any vibration of machinery may have. And then we have to make sure the tunnels are structurally reinforced before we can go on.'

'Of course,' says Dannielle off-screen. 'And at this point, are you any closer to knowing exactly where the children are?'

Seb runs his hand through his hair. 'Well,' he says, 'the good news is that from the information that the last group up have given us we know the collapse occurred just beyond the Evra shaft. Our best information suggests it's maybe a fifteen-to-twenty metre section that has collapsed, which would be far too dangerous to move. So we've descended down another shaft, the other side of the fall. There is still debris, like I said, and it may take longer, but it is the safer option.'

'Well, Seb,' says Dannielle, 'I can see how much effort is going into the search. It must be exhausting.'

'It is,' said Seb, wiping his forehead on his arm. 'But this is the type of thing we train for. We're all doing six-hour shifts, then switching, so the operation can keep going. We've got the best people here to help with the rescue, and of course the amazing fire and ambulance crews. But we are also keeping a watchful eye on the weather.' Seb looks up at the dark sky.

'There have been thunderstorms,' says Dannielle, 'moving in from the east. But the latest forecast suggests they're moving slowly.'

'Let's hope they don't move at all,' says Seb. 'But, listen. We're remaining very positive. The fact that the two instructors made it up gives us great hope that the kids have found a safe place down there.'

Dannielle nods her head. 'We'll let you go now. Try to get some rest.'

'Cheers.' Seb turns away from the camera and walks in the direction of a tent, where more rescuers are gathered.

The screen changes back to the map of the mine network Kate showed us, with the three stick figures deep down at the bottom, where they thought me, Oscar and Effie might be.

'What an amazing person,' says Carly. 'Actually, they're just all amazing people coming together at the same time, with such positivity and hope. Hoping for the best outcome, hoping for a rescue. Here's Dom, and he's got someone with him who was certainly hoping that. I hear she might be quite amazing too.'

The screen switches to Dom, standing in the audience with a microphone.

'Thanks, Carly,' he says. 'That was the situation at the time, but now we're going to have a little chat with six-year-old Lily.' He starts walking down the aisle, stopping two rows behind us in front of a young girl with black hair.

'Lily,' says Dom. 'Tell us a little bit about how you were feeling.'

'Brilliant,' said Lily. 'I got to meet Carly Wyatt!'

'Oh, well, thanks for that!' says Dom, pretending to be hurt.

The audience laughs.

Lily shrugs and gives a cheeky grin. I've seen that shrug and grin a hundred times before. It's just like Oscar's. I look along the row at Oscar, who's holding his head in his hands like he's scared what his sister will say next.

'Actually,' Dom says, 'I meant what were you feeling when you first heard your big brother, Oscar, was down the mine?'

'Don't know, really,' she says, swinging her legs. 'But I was scared because I knew it was serious when both Mum and Dad went. I had to stay with Auntie Gill.'

226

Dom continues, 'Did you think about what Oscar was doing?'

'A bit,' says Lily, 'but I did feel sorry for the others because he can be so annoying.'

The audience laughs again. Oscar holds his face in his hands like he's pretending Lily has nothing to do with him.

I smile. It's great to finally see Lily, after all Oscar said about her when we were in the cave. He was acting like he was embarrassed, but I knew how much he loved her. As the screen goes blank, for a split second I'm back in the cave, listening to him tell us the story of how he went to the circus with her and she was rescued by a clown after accidentally slipping between the seats. For a moment I can hear our laughter again, and how after a while it turned to crying when I told Oscar he should tell his sister he loved her because I'd never told Luke when he was alive. I look at the empty red seat next to me and I wish Effie was sat in it. She knows what the cave was like, she knew the laughter and the tears. If she was here right now, I would hold her hand, and I would squeeze it tight and never let go. *Where is she?* She's missing everything.

Dom Fox walks past me, back up onto the stage.

'Well.' He smiles. 'It seems heroes have very entertaining sisters.'

The audience chuckles, but not for long as a man waves his hand behind the camera, like Dom needs to keep going with the story. I look at Oscar, who takes a deep breath, like he's glad the camera is no longer on Lily. But I know how much he cares about her. I know how much he loves her.

'Have you told her yet?' I mouth.

Oscar shakes his head. 'No,' he says. 'But I will.'

227

CHAPTER 21

WHEN OSCAR'S PHONE DIED / ☹

After the fall came the pain of landing. One shooting through my shoulder, and another piercing my back. I pushed myself up and saw Oscar and Effie standing knee-deep in water.

'Everyone okay?' asked Effie. She was holding her left arm and blood was trickling down her cheek. Oscar waded towards her and put his hand on her shoulder.

'Effie,' he said. 'You all right?'

'Yes,' she said. 'But what about you?' She pointed at the rip in Oscar's jeans, and the blood oozing out.

'Yeah,' replied Oscar.

I shook my head, still dazed as our torches flashed around. We must have tumbled five metres into a well that was draining down a tunnel to my left.

'What do we do now?' I shouted above the roar of the water.

'Get out of here!' yelled Oscar, his voice shrill with fear.

Effie helped me up and we all waded towards another tunnel, me cradling my arm so as not to jar my shoulder. There was no way of knowing this was the right way, only that it was dry.

Another pain shot through my shoulder as I dragged myself up, the sound of tumbling water rushing through my head. Had to get out, had to keep moving, had to stay with Oscar and Effie. More pain jolted through me like an electric shock. I noticed blood trickling down my wet arm.

I kept walking. For the first time in ages it felt like we were going upwards. All I wanted was for the tunnel to keep leading up, up, up, any way up. I felt myself walking faster, keeping my focus on Oscar and Effie. But all the time my shoulder was aching. Every part of me was aching.

We stopped walking as the tunnel widened into a cavern, with two more tunnels branching off it.

Oscar and Effie stopped in the middle. I thought they were deciding which way to go, but they both dropped their bags to the ground.

'I think we need to rest,' Oscar, said, catching his breath. 'At least I do.' Blood was now seeping from both his knees. 'They hurt,' he said, grimacing. 'Worse than when I fell from the top ramp in the skatepark.'

I let my bag fall gently, so as not to jolt my arm. 'Me too,' I said, 'but I'll be okay.'

'What about you, Eff . . . ? Eff?'

We both knelt down beside Effie, who was sat on her bag.

'Yeah,' she said, shivering. 'I think so.' But she didn't look okay. She looked colder, wetter and more bloodied than me and Oscar. And she was shaking, like the shock of nearly drowning was only hitting her now.

'You sure you're all right, Eff?' Oscar asked again.

'Yeah, I am. And it's okay, Oscar, I will say it.'

'What?'

'Thanks for saving my life back there.'

'Big of you to say it.' Oscar grinned.

We were all hurting but still we managed to laugh.

We sat down, looking at our arms and legs, checking them for more cuts and bruises. There was a new gash on my left knee, and the pain in my shoulder was now stabbing like a knife. I looked across at Effie, who was holding up her left arm awkwardly.

'I can't see it,' she said to me. 'Is it cut badly?'

I held her arm gently and saw the blood oozing from her elbow.

'I think we need to cover the cut,' I said. 'Stop the blood coming out.'

'What with?' said Effie, looking round. 'There's not much here to use.'

I looked down at my shirt.

'No, Milo,' said Effie. 'You can't use that.'

'But we need to stop the flow,' I said, pulling my shirt over my head. 'I'll try to tear off an arm, cut it on the edge of a rock.'

'Noooo!' Oscar jumped up, waving his hand in the air. 'It just died!' he yelled. 'My phone just died!'

I stared at the blank screen.

Oscar shook it, like that might make it blip back to life.

'No.' He squirmed like he was in pain. 'No! No! No!'

The three of us stared at the phone in silence. It hadn't had a signal all the time we'd been trapped and we'd only ever used it to keep time. But the moment it actually died, I think we all realised that the phone had given us hope. Hope that any moment it might bleep with a message, or ring and a rescuer would say, 'Hey, we know you're down there,' and 'Don't worry, we're coming!' Or maybe messages from our parents, telling us the sort of things parents say, like 'Be brave and keep going.'

But now Oscar's phone had died, there wouldn't be that little surge of hope we'd all got whenever he checked the screen. There would be no bleep, no voice from the surface.

It didn't matter that it was the latest model.

It didn't matter that the camera had sixteen megapixels.

It didn't matter how much it cost.

Oscar's phone dying extinguished the last spark of hope from our hearts.

Now it was just a useless piece of metal and plastic, sitting in Oscar's hand.

'It must've have been the water,' Effie said quietly.

'Yeah,' I said, looking down at my shirt. 'It must have been.'

Oscar shook his head and said nothing. He didn't have to.

I wished I could say something positive, like we would be okay. I wished Oscar and Effie would say something like that too, but it was like we all felt we had gone so far down that we would never get back up.

I looked at Effie.

'Maybe I won't tear it,' I said, holding up my shirt. 'I'll just tie it round your arm, then have it back when it stops.'

Effie smiled wearily.

'Yeah, Milo,' she said. 'You do that.'

I gently wrapped the arm of my shirt around her elbow, then sat back against the rock. For the first time since we stopped, I noticed the lapping sound of the water echoing off the cave walls. We all knew we had to keep going, but we were so tired, wet and hungry that we just wanted to rest.

'Five minutes,' said Oscar. 'I'll count us five minutes in my head.'

'Yeah,' I said. 'Five minutes. Turn out our lights?'

Effie nodded, even though she no longer had one.

'Yeah,' she said. 'Turn out our lights.'

I clicked off my torch and rested my head back against the rock. My heart thudded heavily. Oscar might have been counting the seconds, but I was counting the beats in my chest.

We had no phone and only one light. How long would that last? When it died, would we be left with nothing but the sound of our breathing and the dark? Always the dark.

I rolled my head against the rock, felt its sharp edges against my skull.

We were so far down.

So far down.

What goes down, must go up.

I smiled.

Ah, Lukey, there you are! I've not heard from you for a while.

You've been a bit busy.

232

Yeah, Lukey, I've been busy.

And you're hurting?

Just a bit. But what were you saying?

That what goes down, must go up? Isn't that what Dad used to say?

No. It was: what goes up must come down.

Isn't that the same thing?

Not really.

Oh.

Dad was talking about gravity, Luke. Like if you throw a ball in the air, it must come down.

But he said it when we were walking up that mountain on holiday. Do you remember?

I do. That was to keep you going. But you're right, he said that if you climb a mountain, it can't go on for ever. At some point you have to reach the top, and then come down the other side.

Like a roller coaster.

Yeah, like a roller coaster.

So this is like a roller coaster, only we're going down. Down, down, down. But then we hit the bottom and go up the other side.

I sighed.

That would be good, Lukey. Thanks for trying to cheer me up.

That's okay. I got a name for it.

For what?

Our roller coaster.

Go on.

Journey to the centre of the earth!

I smiled.

Yeah, just like the film. 'Journey to the centre of the
earth' is good, Lukey.

*Cool, and if we don't go up the other side, then we just
keep going and we'll come out in Australia. There might
not be any lions, but there'll be kangaroos.*

I chuckled.

That can't happen. But I like the idea.

So you'll keep going?

What?

You'll keep going. Get out us out of here?

I imagined the words coming out of Luke's mouth. I imagined him
grinning as he brushed his blond hair out of his eyes. The gap between
his front teeth, the little brown mole on his left cheek. It was like he
was sat right next to me. So close, so warm, I wanted to reach out and
hug him. I'd not heard from him in a while but now his words were
still going through my head, over and over, like a talking Action Man
toy stuck on repeat.

You'll keep going and get us out of here?
You'll keep going and get us out of here?

'Yeah, Lukey,' I said. 'Yeah, we –'

'Milo,' Oscar switched his torch on, 'you're doing that talking thing again. It's freaking me out.'

I squinted in the light.

'Just talking to myself,' I said, searching for an answer.

'Really? Since when have you called yourself Lukey? Wait, isn't that your brother's name?'

I glanced at Effie, thinking she might help me out, but she just sighed.

'Milo,' she said, 'I think it's time you told him. I think it's time you told everyone. If you don't now, you might not ever.'

'Tell me what?' said Oscar.

Effie squeezed my arm.

'Go on, Milo,' she said. 'You know you should.'

I took a deep breath. I'd buried my secret so deep, it had a long way to come out.

'Milo?' Oscar's face was up close to mine.

'Okay,' I said. 'Okay … you're right, the person I was talking to was my brother.'

'And?'

'And … well … he's … he's …'

'He's?'

'Well, he's …'

'Dead?' asked Oscar.

I swallowed hard. Luke had been gone for nearly a year, and still the *D*-word wouldn't come out of my mouth.

'Yeah,' I said. 'He's that.'

'Wow!' Oscar blew his cheeks out. 'I mean ... I mean, Wow!'

'Oscar!' Effie scowled.

'What?' Oscar turned to her. 'Wait ... you already knew.'

'Yeah,' Effie said quietly.

I waited for Oscar to snap, tell Effie that she should have told him, or tell me that he knew I was weird. But he just blew his cheeks out again.

'So you talk to him ... like ... Is he a ghost?'

'No,' I said. 'He's with me all the time ... in my head.'

'Well,' Oscar smiled, 'I guess that must be quite fun.'

Effie laughed. 'Oscar,' she said, 'sometimes you should engage your brain before you speak.'

'What?' said Oscar. 'It's okay for you, I only just found out ... Wait!' His face lit up ... So that's why you're here?'

'Oscar!' snapped Effie.

'It's okay,' I said. 'But yes, that's why I'm here.'

'Well, I think it's quite cool,' said Oscar. 'Not that he's ... you know ... I mean, if I had a, you know, brother, I'd talk to him too.'

Aww, that's nice.

'Did you want to talk about it now, Milo?' asked Effie.

'Course he does,' said Oscar. 'Don't you, Milo? What sort of stuff do you chat to him about?'

I'd dreaded telling anyone about Luke, especially Oscar, but now the secret was out, it suddenly became easier to talk.

'Everything,' I said. 'How we used to play football in the garden and when we took our kite to the park, but mostly I just like that he's there.'

Even if you have forgotten about me lately.

I haven't. I promise I haven't.

'Wait,' said Oscar, like he could see the worry on my face. 'Is he there now?'

'Yeah,' I said. 'I told you, he's always there.'

'Maybe it's more that you imagine what he would say,' said Effie, as if she'd noticed Oscar was thinking I was totally weird. 'I know my nan so well that I can imagine what she would say if she was with me.'

'Like confloption,' I said.

'Yeah.' Effie smiled. 'Like confloption.'

'What does that mean?' asked Oscar.

'Just a made-up word my nan uses,' said Effie. 'For when things have gone wrong or are a mess.'

'Confloption.' Oscar nodded. 'Yeah, I like that. What other things do you imagine she would say?'

'Lots of things,' said Effie. 'And it's not just what she says. When you love someone, you think of them all the time.'

'Hmm,' said Oscar. 'I can't say I think about anybody.'

'Then maybe you should let people get to know you better,' said Effie.

'Well, yeah,' said Oscar, picking up his bag. 'Anyway, I prefer that Milo actually has his brother in his head. Which way does he say we should go, Milo?' He was avoiding talking about himself again and putting the attention back on me.

I shrugged. Luke had told me to keep going, but not which way.

'How about we vote?' said Oscar. 'That way we all celebrate if things go right, and no one gets the blame if it goes wrong.'

'Blimey,' said Effie, 'that's almost sensible. What's come over you?'

'Nothing,' said Oscar. 'But people can change, you know. And I think it's a fair way,' he continued. 'There can't ever be a draw as there's three of us.'

Four!
Sorry, Luke. Your vote doesn't count.
Bit unfair.
It's okay, I'll let you share mine.
Oh, cool.
Just as long as you agree with me.
What? No!

'So,' said Oscar. 'Now that's sorted, we'll do the first vote. What idiot votes for going down there, where the water flows in, and if we go back, we'll probably drown?'

'Well,' said Effie, carefully hitching her bag onto her shoulder. 'It's such a hard decision, Oscar, when you put it like that.'

'So we're going that way, yeah?' Oscar pointed. 'And before I

238

forget, we also take it in turns to lead. That way we third our chances of being the first one to fall down a hole.'

'There,' said Effie. 'That's the Oscar I know!'

We all laughed. The situation was still serious, but it was like Effie's joke had cracked ten-metre-thick ice.

We picked up our bags and me and Effie followed Oscar down the tunnel. I was glad I'd told Oscar about Luke, but as we walked on, there was still something on my mind. Something that Luke had just said to me, that he thought I'd forgotten about him.

Do you really think that, Lukey? Do you really think I
would forget you?
Well . . .
Do you?
Yeah, just a little bit. But it's okay.
No, Lukey. It's never okay.

CHAPTER 22

OUR LIVES ARE A FILM /
CAN I BE IN IT?

It was like a weight had been lifted off me as we all crouched and squeezed through the gaps. And Oscar had cheered up too, once he figured that his phone dying meant his dad would buy him a new one, which made Effie laugh again. But not as much as when he started talking about what it would be like when he went back to school.

'Just imagine,' he said. 'Everyone will want to speak to us because we've been on the news. I bet the reporters have been to our schools and interviewed our friends. I hope they speak to my best friend, Ryan. He knows all the cool stuff about me.'

'There's cool stuff about you?' said Effie.

I chuckled.

'Milo,' Oscar shouted back to me. 'How is it you don't say much but you know when to laugh?'

I laughed again.

'I don't know,' I shouted back. 'Just do.'

'Anyway, who would you two pick to talk about you on TV . . . And you can't have your mum or dad.'

'That's easy,' said Effie.

'Can't be your nan, either,' said Oscar. 'Although she would say this was a confluxion.'

'Confloption,' said Effie. 'Get it right.'

'Confloption,' said Oscar. 'What a confloption.'

I smiled. Talking with Oscar and Effie this way was like finding games to play on a long journey, only we had no cars to guess the colour of, and no clouds to spot. All we had was our memories and imagination.

'So, go on, then,' Oscar shouted again. 'Who would you have? Actually, I just thought, I hope Ryan doesn't say anything about skiving off school together. My mum and dad don't know anything about that. Maybe it should be my other best friend, Guia. She'll say nice things, like she misses me sitting next to her in Science and that she can't wait for me to get back.'

'Blimey,' said Effie. 'How many "best friends" have you got? I've counted a dozen since we've been down here.'

'I can't help it if I'm popular,' said Oscar. 'Actually, come to think of it, I've got so many they could make a whole series about me on Netflix, and when we get out, you two can come round my house and we can binge-watch it.'

'Oh yeah,' said Effie, looking back at me. 'Can't wait for that.'

I laughed.

'See?' shouted Oscar. 'He's laughing again. So come on, Milo. Oh no, I forgot. You don't have any friends.'

'Oscar!' Effie shouted.

'Nah, didn't mean it, Milo. You know I didn't. Maybe your mum and dad would just hand over one of your stories and they'd read it out on TV. Blimey, they might even turn it into a book. Milo, get this, you might be a millionaire author by the time we get out.'

'I wish,' I said, shaking my head. A few days before, I might have been upset by Oscar poking fun, but now he knew me better, now I knew him, everything was fine. So fine that for once I could think of a reply.

'Maybe I'll write one about you, Oscar,' I said. 'In fact, all of us. A story about us all down here in the mine.'

'Yeah,' said Effie, 'maybe we could be archaeologists, looking for buried treasure.'

'Or scientists,' said Oscar. 'We've invented something that can save the Earth, and we've hidden it in a mine, so no one else can get it.'

'Could do,' I said. 'I'd write about any of that just as long as I could write the words "WE GOT OUT!"'

'Yeah.' Oscar's laugh echoed back to me, then suddenly stopped. 'Oh no!' He pointed down the tunnel.

'What?' me and Effie said at the same time.

Oscar dropped his bag to the ground.

'It's a dead end!'

AWARDS FOR HEROES

The big screen flashes with lightning as Carly Wyatt walks onto the stage. 'It was about now that things started to change,' she shouts above the rumble of thunder. 'As you can see from the footage of the lightning filmed at the time, a storm had arrived. Thunder, lightning and torrents of rain. These pictures show how the tracks and paths had turned to rivers. And of course, with it that bad up on the surface, there were now real concerns for the water levels down in the cave, in the area where rescuers believed the children might be.'

'A very serious situation.' Dom Fox takes over. 'More fire engines had arrived, along with sandbags and pumps. The idea was to use them to divert the water away from the immediate area, and the water that did get through would be pumped out. But as you can see it was almost monsoon-like weather.'

My body shakes as the thunder rumbles from the speakers. I glance across at Oscar and see the lights from the fire engines flashing his face blue. He's sitting open-mouthed, like the storm and the police cars and the fire engines have arrived right here, right now, inside the arena.

Too loud.

Too bright.

I wish they would turn the sound down.

I wish they would switch off the screen.

I put my hands over my ears. Oscar does the same.

'Too much,' he mouths. 'Too much.'

Back on the screen, the rescue team and the firefighters are clearing a path as they unravel the hoses from the pumps and trail them across the dust which has now turned to mud.

Then we see all the people, all our mums and dads and Effie's nan, sheltering in tents, waiting for news, while the reporters and the camera people wait outside.

The drone of the pumps.

The flashes of lightning.

The rumble of thunder.

The sound of people shouting.

The rain falling.

Oscar is right – this is too much.

I press my hands harder against my ears and close my eyes. All those things were happening on the surface while me, Oscar and Effie were trapped a hundred metres below.

CHAPTER 23

NO WAY OUT / *THE END*

A wall of rock ahead of us.

Water creeping along the tunnel behind us. It didn't matter which way we looked, or how many times we swivelled our heads from side to side.

We were trapped within a trap.

No way forward.

No way back.

For a while we sat in silence, sometimes looking at each other, anxiously smiling, trying to make each other feel better, at other times looking away, like we didn't want to make eye contact, in case we were all thinking the same thing . . .

But we still had each other. We still had our hopes and dreams.

Oscar said he wanted to join the army, drive a tank, have armour built into his body to make him indestructible. He'd seen it in a documentary, or maybe he'd dreamed it or seen it in a film. Either way it didn't matter; he was going to be so strong and tough that he was going to save the world.

Effie said she just wanted to stay near her nan. She would leave home, but she liked the idea of having lots of sheep and cows and living close by on a farm. Or maybe a vet, yeah, she'd like to be a vet, take care of animals.

And I didn't know what I wanted to do, because since Luke had died I hadn't looked a day ahead, let alone years. But when I thought about it, when I really thought about it, I knew I wanted to be a writer, to make people laugh and cry at the things I wrote. And I promised Oscar and Effie I would write about us, and maybe if the book was good it would sell millions of copies, and we'd see it in bookshop windows and maybe we could all meet up at a red-carpet premiere when it was made into a film.

Oscar loved that part.

Effie too.

And all the time the water was getting closer, lapping up the tunnel, sucking away our air

But I wasn't giving up.

None of us were giving up, even though the cave felt colder and darker than it ever had before.

I might have said I wanted to be a writer, but right at that moment all I wanted to do was go home and cuddle on the sofa with Mum and Dad while we told each other stories about Luke. But the only person I could hug now was myself, and no matter how tightly I wrapped my arms around myself I couldn't stop shaking.

I felt Effie's hand on my arm, in the dark.

'Milo . . .' she whispered. 'I'm so cold.'

'I know,' I said, still shivering. 'Me too.'

'And me,' said Oscar. 'I can't feel my hands or my feet.' He knelt closer, so close I could feel his legs shaking against mine.

'Group hug?' said Effie.

I opened my arms. For the first time in nearly a year, I didn't need to be asked to hug someone. I did it because I wanted to, and it felt like the most natural thing in the whole world.

I opened my arms and pulled Oscar and Effie towards me. Our heads bumped gently together.

This is nice.
Yeah.

My coat was wet through, but it didn't matter. I took it off. Effie and Oscar wrapped their arms around me, and I lifted my coat and covered us all.

'You dare tell anyone about this,' whispered Oscar.

'Wouldn't dream of it,' said Effie. 'Why would I want to tell anyone I hugged you?'

We all tried to laugh, but only shaky giggles came out.

'We've got to hold on,' said Effie. 'Someone will come. I know they will.'

We all went quiet, like we were hoping that was true, but couldn't help wondering if it wasn't.

We hugged each other tighter.

'Tell us a story, Milo,' said Oscar.

A sucking sound echoed off the tunnel walls.

We all looked at each other. For a while we'd forgotten about the water, because what was the point in thinking about it anyway?

It's like a monster.

Yeah.

And it's coming to get us.

I looked at Oscar and Effie. None of us spoke, we just stared back down the tunnel, waiting for the water to arrive, knowing that once it did, there was no escape.

'Okay. Story,' I said.

'And Luke can listen too,' said Oscar.

'Of course.' I smiled, even though it felt like this was the last story I would ever tell. I hated to think that there would be no one left to tell Luke stories when I was gone. In fact, if he was no longer in my mind, he might not exist at all.

I took a deep breath.

'You would have liked him,' I said. 'My brother, Luke. You would have liked him.'

'I know I would.' Effie held me tighter.

'Yeah,' said Oscar. 'Me too.'

We all tensed as cold water lapped over our trainers, over our legs.

I think you should start now.

Yeah, I think I should.

Your new one, the boy on the iceberg.

It's not finished.

But you could finish it now. I could help.

'Come on, Milo,' said Oscar.

'Okay,' I said. 'Okay . . .' The water was filling the cave around us. If I didn't start the story now, I would never finish.

I cleared my throat.

'Once there was a boy who was lost on an iceberg. He was all alone, except for a polar bear and two seals.

And his brother?

'. . . And his brother.'

They were called Luke and Milo.

'Their names were Luke and Milo, and while they waited to be rescued, they played computer games on a giant sheet of ice that shot up, as if by magic, out of the water. It was as tall as two double-decker buses, and just as wide.'

Cool.

'Cool,' said Oscar. 'I'd love that.'

'Of course you would,' said Effie. 'What about the polar bear and seals, Milo?'

'Oh.' I smiled. 'They sometimes played too, but mostly they caught fish for the boys to eat.'

Effie and Oscar laughed.

'What next?' asked Effie.

'After three days on the iceberg, fearing they would never get recued, the boys saw the silhouette of a ship sailing towards them in the fog.'

I paused as the water pooled around my waist and stole my breath.

I think we should skip to the good part.

I think we should skip.

I think we should.

I think . . .

I closed my eyes. Suddenly I was so scared that I could no longer speak, but the story kept going in my head.

The ship arrived and the little boy jumped up and asked the captain where he was going. He hoped it was somewhere warm, like Spain or Brazil.

Disneyland!

Ha! Yeah, Disneyland.

The little boy climbed up the ladder at the side of the boat and told the captain to take him away.

No, that's not what happens. The boys always
stay together.
*The little boy stands on the deck beside the captain
and waves goodbye.*
No, he doesn't. Luke, what are you doing? This is my
story, our story.
*It's okay. The little boy is okay. He tells his brother he
doesn't have to look after him any more.*
Lukey, stop it. I know what you're trying to say. But I like
looking after you. Always have, always will.
*And I like it too, Milo, but I think it's time you looked
after yourself. Because I'm happy.*
What does that mean . . . Luke, what does that mean?
I'm happy. Happy, happy, happy.
Luke! No . . . Luke! The little boy waves again as
the boat's engine rumbles, its hull cracking through
the icebergs.
Bye, Milo!

'No, Lukey! No! Don't go! Don't . . .'

'Milo! Milo!'

I opened my eyes.

Oscar grabbed my arm and pulled me up.

'Did you feel that?' he yelled. 'Milo, please tell me you felt that!'

'We can't have imagined it. Just wait, listen again,' said Effie.

I hadn't heard a thing. All I knew was that the water was up to
our chests.

251

A rumbling sound vibrated through the rock.

'There!' said Effie, holding up her hand. 'Did you hear that?

The cave rumbled again, like thunder.

We all looked up, like at any moment we expected the rocks to fall down on top of us.

We turned on our lights.

'It's coming from that direction,' said Oscar, pointing. 'I'm pretty sure . . .'

Water splashed around us as we edged our way back down the tunnel.

'Hello!' Oscar shouted. 'Hello, is anyone there?'

A rock fell from the wall ahead of us.

Effie held her arm out. 'I think we should stay here,' she said. 'It doesn't look safe.'

'Hello!' Oscar yelled again. 'Is anyone there?'

'Hello!' A woman's shout came back, stopping us dead in our tracks.

Oscar's face cracked into a grin.

'They're here!' he shouted. 'What did I tell you?'

Another piece of rock tumbled down in front of us.

'Oscar, Effie, Milo, can you hear me?' called the voice.

'Yes!' we shouted at the same time.

'Stay exactly where you are. Don't come down the tunnel. Not until we get through and drain this water away.'

We all looked at each other. I wanted to hug them and cheer, but the woman sounded so cautious.

'Just keep back,' she said.

Another chunk of rock tumbled down, then a beam of light shone into the tunnel.

Oscar wrapped one arm around my shoulder and the other around Effie.

'We made it.' He grinned. 'We're going to be okay.'

The beam of light grew wider, from a small hole to the size of my bedroom window. Then suddenly it was blocked out, as a woman wearing a hard hat and a high-vis jacket scrambled through. She stood up and looked down the tunnel at us.

'Stay there,' she said, holding up her hand. 'Just for a moment while we make this safe.'

We all nodded at the same time, like just speaking might make the rocks fall down.

'Are any of you hurt?' asked the woman.

'A little bit,' said Effie. 'We've all got cuts and bruises. Milo's arm is quite bad, but I don't think it's broken.'

'That's good,' said the woman.

Another rock rolled down. I looked down and saw the water was starting to run away.

'Have you got this, Hal?'

'Yep, all good, Chloe. You go on down.'

A red bag was pushed through the hole.

Chloe took it, then walked towards us.

'Well,' she said, smiling. 'Haven't you three had an adventure?'

'You could say that,' said Oscar, looking at me and Effie.

'Yeah, just a bit of one,' said Effie.

'And you, Milo?'

'Yeah,' I said, suddenly starting to shake. I wanted to celebrate and cry at the same time. One minute I thought the cave was falling in, the next a team of rescuers were coming through a hole.

I looked at Oscar and Effie. They were shivering too.

'Here,' said Chloe, reaching into the bag. 'Put these on.' She passed us silver capes like I'd seen in *Mountain Rescue* on TV. 'Just try to get warm,' said Chloe, 'then we'll check you over before taking you back up to the surface.'

I wrapped the foil around myself and hugged it tight under my chin. Effie and Oscar did the same.

'You dare say anything about chickens.' Oscar grinned.

'Wouldn't,' I said, trying to stop my teeth chattering. 'Couldn't.'

Effie smiled, but as Kate searched through her bag, I felt that me, Oscar and Effie all had the same question on our minds. It looked like we were safe but what about the others? We wanted to know, but only if it was good, not if they had been buried under the rubble.

It was Effie who managed to get her words out first.

'Are the others okay?' she asked. 'Matty and Lois ... and the others. They were right behind us.'

'They're fine,' said Chloe, handing us energy bars to eat, and bidons of water. 'It took a while, but they're fine.'

Effie smiled with relief.

'So we've been down here the longest?' said Oscar, like he was pleased.

'Yes,' said Chloe.

'Cool,' said Oscar.

Effie shook her head.

'What?' said Oscar. 'Just being honest. Means we get all the attention on TV. Isn't that right, Milo?'

I laughed with relief. I didn't care about being on TV or being famous. All I cared about was that help had arrived to get us out. It all seemed to be happening so quickly, as two more rescuers had now come through the hole and were arranging ropes across the cave floor.

'It's going to take a while to get you back up,' said Chloe. 'You've come a long way down, but me, Hal and Neville will pair up with you, and guide you through. Just pop these on.'

'You're Milo?' asked Hal.

I nodded and he placed a harness over my head, then fastened it over my chest.

'Just clip that on the rope,' he said holding up a hook.

I clipped the hook on. It was similar to the one I'd used on the zip-wire. Only this time we weren't going down, but up.

'Okay,' said Chloe. 'We're all ready?'

'Yep,' said Hal and Neville.

'Yep,' said Oscar and Effie.

I nodded.

'Great,' said Chloe. 'Let's go.'

CHAPTER 24

UP!

My mind was a blur as Hal and Neville led us through the narrow twisty bits, then pulled us over ledges, with Chloe following us. Hal kept asking if we were okay. I couldn't tell him what I was thinking. In fact, I couldn't say anything at all, unlike Oscar who seemed to be talking all the way.

'Are there cameras?' he asked. 'Reporters and stuff?'

'Yeah,' said Hal. 'But it's okay, we'll try to keep you away from them. Go somewhere quiet where we can check you over and you can see your mum and dad.'

'No way!' said Oscar. 'I didn't get stuck down here just to go to a quiet room. I'll talk to them. I'll answer their questions. I mean, who doesn't want to be on TV? All my friends will be watching. I'll be famous.'

'Well, at least one of you seems okay,' said Chloe.

'Yeah,' said Oscar. 'Just blimmin' hungry. Have you got anything else to eat?'

Effie laughed behind me. 'Yeah, he's fine. We've had to put up with that for two days, haven't we, Milo?'

I smiled when she said my name. It felt like it was her way of checking if I was okay.

'Yeah,' I replied. 'It was pretty much non-stop.'

'It was not,' said Oscar. 'Well, maybe I did go on a little bit.'

'Just a little bit,' said Effie quietly, which made everyone laugh, even if it was nervously. I was hungry too. And I was relieved to have been found, but I knew this wasn't over until we were actually out.

I started to imagine what it would be like to see daylight again. To see the sun.

To see the sky.

And to see planes.

Effie saw it first. I'd expected a shout, even a scream, but she just stopped dead and I heard her whisper, 'There it is. There it is.'

I peered past her, and there, maybe ten metres away, I saw it too: a bright shaft of light, shining down, like a spaceship had landed above.

I waited for Oscar to shout something like, 'We've made it! I told you so,' but after so long waiting, wishing, hoping to find something, we were so shocked that we walked towards it in silence, like we thought the spaceship would lift off and leave us alone any second.

'This is one of the old ventilation shafts,' said Neville, 'so it's pretty narrow, but don't worry, we'll just have to take you up one by one.'

I looked at Oscar and Effie. After being together for so long, I just wanted us to stay that way.

'We'll be okay,' said Effie like she was thinking the same. 'We can wait for each other at the top, can't we?'

'Of course,' said Chloe. 'We'll keep you together, if that's what you want.'

Oscar nodded quickly.

'Yeah,' he said. 'That's what we want.'

'Great,' said Chloe. 'So who wants to go—'

'Me,' said Oscar, before Chloe could finish speaking.

Me and Effie laughed. For someone who said he was cool and not scared, Oscar suddenly couldn't wait another second to get out.

'Is that okay with you two?'

'Yes,' me and Effie said at the same time.

'But I will wait for you, yeah?' said Oscar. 'Like we said, at the top.'

'Yeah,' Effie and I said, in unison again.

Hal stepped forward. 'Ready, Oscar?' he said. 'I just need to fasten you in, then we'll get winched up.'

Oscar nodded and watched Hal as he attached a metal clip to his harness. We were now so close to getting out that even Oscar had run out of words.

Chloe's walkie-talkie crackled.

She pressed the button.

'Yep,' she said. 'Hal and Oscar are coming up now.'

'Just hold on to me,' said Hal. 'Elbows in and try your best to keep still.'

'Okay,' said Oscar, then his eyes opened wide as the rope went taut.

'Laters.' He grinned.

'Yeah,' Effie said. 'Laters.'

Slowly Hal and Oscar were lifted into the air. Hal with one arm out, pushing against the rock, like he was trying to stop them both spinning round. Effie came and stood beside me.

'It won't be long now, Milo,' she said.

'No,' I said as Oscar and Hal went up the shaft, blocking the light. And for a moment it was dark again.

'I know I'm a long way from you, but we could message, maybe video-chat. So I know you're okay.'

'Yeah,' I said. 'That would be nice. That way I know you're okay too.'

Effie smiled. 'I'm always okay, Milo. You know that?'

'Yes,' I said. 'I know you are.'

Oscar and Hal reached the top and the light shone brightly down the shaft once more.

'All clear,' came the message on the walkie-talkie.

'Okay,' said Chloe. 'Who's next?'

Effie nodded at me.

'He is,' she said. And I knew it was pointless to argue.

Chloe smiled. 'We'll let Neville take you up, Milo. That okay?'

I stepped forward. Neville clipped me onto his harness.

'Just say if anything worries you,' he said calmly. 'We'll take it easy.'

'Okay,' I replied, then my heart started thudding as the rope went taut.

'See you at the top,' Effie said.

'Yeah,' I replied. 'See you at the top.'

CHAPTER 25

WHITE LIGHTS

White lights.

Bright white lights.

That was the moment we were safe.

The most amazing moment of my life.

But all I can remember are the lights.

Bright white lights.

No words.

No feelings.

Numb.

The thing I'd most wanted, for two days, the moment I had looked forward to, yet all I could see was white lights.

Too bright.

Too bright.

I put my hand over my eyes.

'Milo, can you tell us how you feel?'

'Milo, can you describe what it was like?'

'Milo, have you got anything to say to the rescuers who helped you make it back out?'

Then black.

Black.

Black.

My body and brain shut down.

Like I was a computer, and someone had pulled out the plug.

'The doctors are very happy with you,' Mum said. 'They just want to keep an eye on you for the rest of the night. We're going to stay with you, then we'll take you home in the morning. Okay?'

'Yeah,' I said. 'Okay.'

'You sure?' asked Mum. 'Only you don't look it. Is there something bothering you? A pain you've not told us about?'

'No,' I said. 'I'm fine.'

'If you're worried about Effie and Oscar,' said Dad, 'they seem to be fine too, but the doctors think you should all rest, and you can meet up before we leave tomorrow.'

'Okay,' I said, resting my head back on my pillow. I was aching all over – my shoulder, my elbow, my knees – but the biggest ache of all was in my heart. I didn't want Oscar and Effie to leave. They had become my friends down there in the dark, and even though Mum and Dad were with me, I felt like I was on my own.

'Couldn't you take me to see them?' I asked. 'Just for a few moments, so I know they are okay.'

'We did ask,' said Dad, looking at Mum, 'but they're still being checked out, and they need to be with their families too.'

'In the morning, love,' Mum said, smoothing my hair. 'When you're all more comfortable.'

I sighed, but as soon as I closed my eyes the darkness hit me again. And I saw the rocks tumbling down, the cave walls closing in. I opened my eyes, stared up at the light on the ceiling, and felt like I would never be able to sleep again.

'It was horrible,' I said. 'Horrible.'

'We know,' said Mum. 'We know.'

The light began to blur. I felt tears trickling down the side of my face.

Mum leaned over the bed, but suddenly I felt trapped. By her, by Dad, by the sheets on my bed.

My legs began to twitch.

'No,' I said. 'Too close, you're too close, I can't breathe.'

They both stepped back. I sat up and pulled the sheets off me.

'I need to get out,' I said. 'I need to . . .' My voice cracked. I wanted to get out but there was nowhere I wanted to go.

Mum cautiously put her arm around my shoulder.

I took a deep breath, then another.

'I'll go find a nurse,' Dad said.

'No,' I said. 'Get Oscar, get Effie.' I began to sob. I'd been out of the mine for nearly two hours, but now it was hitting me, as hard as the rocks when they began to fall.

I lay back on my bed.

'Milo,' whispered Mum, 'everything will be fine. Everything will be . . .'

She stopped talking as doctors and nurses in blue-and-white

uniforms came in.

'Take it easy, Milo,' said one. 'Try to relax. Don't worry, we're going to give you something just to calm you down.'

I felt Mum's smooth hand on my forehead, another on my shoulder, then she lowered me back gently onto the bed.

I stared up at the light.

Something was missing. Someone was missing, but it wasn't Oscar, or Effie ... Lukey. I'd not spoken to him for ages, not since our last story in the mine.

Lukey?

'Lukey,' I said.

The lights began to blur.

'Relax, love. Relax. Talk in the morning.'

Lukey ... where are you?

I waited, waited, waited, through the evening and into the night for Luke to come back.

Dark shadows of nurses came to check on me.

Then I heard whispers by the door.

'He seems more settled now.'

'He seems more stable.'

Then the door opened, and light came in.

The light faded.

The door shut.

On my own again.

Just the click of footsteps out in the corridor.

A ringing phone in the reception area.

Beep. Beep. Beep.

Machines beeping somewhere.

Beep. Beep. Beep.

I'm sorry, Lukey. I'm sorry I can't stop the beeps.
I know that's why you're gone.

I'll find you tomorrow. Okay?

Yes. I'll find you at home tomorrow. Yeah.

The door opens.

Light comes in.

Another shadow.

Beep. Beep. Beep.

The door closes.

The light fades.

On my own again.

Is this what it was like, Luke?

Was it?

I waited.

Waited.

Waited.

But still there was no answer.

Just one big hole, where Luke used to be.

CHAPTER 26

THE GOODBYES

The next morning, I finally got to meet with Oscar and Effie again. I wanted to be alone with them, in a quiet room, where we could talk about what had happened and remember how we had felt. I wanted to laugh and joke with them, to try to make the serious things funny, but most of all, I wanted to tell them about Luke.

I thought maybe talking about him with them would make him come back. But I never got the chance to find out because the room was full of people – my mum and dad, Oscar's mum, Effie's nan and some doctors and nurses from the hospital, all standing around drinking tea and eating biscuits. Oscar, Effie and I looked at each other awkwardly. While we were in the mine, it had felt like we were best friends that no one could ever pull apart. Now it was like we'd turned up at the wrong school and didn't know each other or any of the other kids there.

I tried to talk to Effie when we were standing at a table getting some juice, but since Luke had gone missing from my head it was like I'd lost my voice again. Or maybe it was just that it had been so

266

much easier talking to her in the dark. It was weird, but the mine had become my safe place to talk, and with so many people around I felt like I wanted to go back down there again.

After about an hour, Oscar finally got his wish of becoming famous. The hospital had arranged for all the reporters and TV people to meet us in another room. Even though Effie told me I would be okay, that she would stay with me, I didn't want to be interviewed. Instead I watched from the doorway, as the cameras flashed, and Oscar answered most of the questions, saying things like, 'No, I wasn't scared,' and, 'Yes, I always knew we'd get out.' And Effie glanced at me, like we both knew that wasn't true. But part of me wished I could be like Oscar, because it was like the only scars he had from being down the mine were the nicks and scratches on his face. My scars felt much deeper than that.

'We'll message, yeah?' Oscar said, as we all stood in the car park afterwards. 'Keep chatting.'

'Yeah.' Effie nodded. 'That's if you still want to talk to us, now you're so famous,' she added.

'Oh, I think I'll manage that.' Oscar smiled. 'I'll squeeze you in in between being on the news and my own TV show.'

Effie laughed, but all I could manage was a tired smile.

'You too, Milo.' Oscar put his hand on my shoulder, like he had noticed. 'We'll message, yeah? Maybe you can all come and stay at my house.'

'Or ours,' said Effie's nan.

'That would be nice,' said my mum. 'Wouldn't it, Milo?'

I nodded, trying to think of something else to say, but it was like

Mum was speaking for me once more. I was back to being quiet Milo. The Milo who didn't do hugs, the Milo who was made of stone. But I did want to hug. I wanted to hug Oscar and Effie, but it felt weird in the middle of a car park with the adults around.

The car was full of silence on the way home. Interrupted only by Mum and Dad saying things like how much they had missed me, how they had worried, I must be hungry, what would I like for lunch. But I didn't feel like eating. All I wanted was to get back to our house, so I could find Luke again.

When I got in I went straight up to my bedroom, then Luke's room, then our den in the garage, calling his name over and over again in my head.

Luke.

Luke?

Lukey!

But the only reply was the sound of my own breath.

And then I went round the whole house again like I was looking for a lost cat.

Dad tried to help. He didn't know what I was looking for, only that something was up. 'Do you want to play football?' he asked. 'I'll even go in goal.' But that just made things worse, because I'd not kicked a ball in the garden since Luke had gone. The bare grass where the goal was had turned green.

Mum cooked my favourite tea of fish fingers, chips and mushy peas. But I felt so sick with worry that I just pushed the food around my plate.

Did I want to go on my PlayStation?

Did I want to play a boardgame?

Did I just want to sit quietly and watch TV?

No, all I wanted to do was go to my room and wait for it to get dark.

Because there was one more thing I could do to try and get Luke back. Something I knew he could never resist, no matter how bad or scared he might be feeling.

Luke loved the lion.

He'd come back for that.

That night I waited for Mum and Dad to click off their bedroom light.

Then I waited for a while longer, just in case one of them got up again to go to the toilet or realised they had forgotten to switch off the TV from the socket downstairs.

Nothing.

Another ten minutes, just to be sure.

I think it's safe now, Lukey?

Yeah, I think it's safe.

I reached down by my side and got our book out of my drawer.

Shall we start again, Lukey?

Still not there?

Yeah, I think we'll start again.

I swung my legs over the side of the bed and picked up my phone. If this was going to work, I had to read the book properly, by torchlight, sitting on our beanbag in the wardrobe.

Like we used to. Just Luke and me.

I put my hand on the wardrobe door and pulled it open.

Slowly, slowly. We can't wake Mum and Dad.

Why did the chicken ... Ha, that's what you'd normally say. And you can if you want.

But I didn't just want Luke's voice back, I wanted him there for real, in his Spider-Man pyjamas, with bits of toothpaste smeared white around his big grin.

Imagine that, I told myself. *Just imagine it.*

The door was now open. My clothes hung on the rack. Our beanbag sat underneath.

Is there really another world in our wardrobe?
Of course.

The wood creaked as I climbed in and closed the door behind me.

This is nice, isn't it, Lukey?

Yes, this is nice.

The beanbag rustled as I wriggled to get comfortable.

You good?

I'm good.

I opened our book.

Ready?

Ready ... 'Once there was a boy, a girl and a ...'

Not going to say it, Lukey?

No? No lion ...? Once there was a boy, a girl and a lion, and this is the story of how they all came to meet, in the middle of the Amazon ... Can we skip to the good part?

Luke?

Lukey? No chicken?

There was no lion, no good part.

And there was no chicken joke.

It was just me and my book, in my wardrobe. All on my own.

CHAPTER 27

TWO MONTHS LATER

AWARDS FOR HEROES

I didn't know what to say when Mum told me she'd got an email from the Awards for Heroes people. I thought maybe it was an event where we'd all get together to thank Chloe and Hal and all the other rescuers who were down the mine that day. They were the true heroes, not us. But that wasn't my only thought about the event. Mum tried to make it sound it exciting, telling me, 'We'll buy you a new suit, and a bright tie, maybe stay in a nice hotel in London, go on the London Eye again.' But it didn't matter what she said, because I didn't want a new suit, and going to the London Eye without Luke wouldn't be the same. But most of all, after just two months, I still didn't feel ready to meet people again.

'People cope with trauma in different ways.' That's what the counsellor, Diara, told me, Oscar and Effie in our first online session. 'Some people bottle it all up because they find it too much to talk about. Some people carry on like nothing has happened. But what happened to you, being down in the mine, will have an effect on all of you. You just don't know when that will happen. We just need to make sure we all keep talking. So I think that's what we should do.'

Oscar and Effie nodded.

'So, for example,' Diara continued, 'it's natural to feel anxious in certain situations. Even something as normal as going out into the garden, or walking to the shops.'

'I googled it,' said Oscar. 'There were some kids in Australia who fell down a sinkhole, and for months afterwards two of them wouldn't go outside because they thought the ground would open up and swallow them. How crazy is that?'

'Not crazy,' said Diara. 'Not crazy at all.'

'Well, it is,' said Oscar. 'Just a bit.'

Effie smiled into her camera, and I wished she was with me in person, not two hundred miles away, as we did our counselling sessions on a computer screen.

In the second session, the week after, Diara asked us questions and suggested topics for us to discuss, like how we were finding school since the new term had started, and how we were coping now the TV news reporters weren't around. Effie mostly said that everything was normal now she was back with her friends, and she hadn't really liked being on TV anyway. Whereas Oscar said he was missing waking up and seeing all the reporters and news vans outside. But he was happy because he'd been given a free pair of walking boots and *Caving Monthly* had put him on the front cover of their magazine.

Most of the time I was happy to let everyone else do the talking. It was hard enough to think of anything to say without Luke prompting me. But it was even harder just sitting in my bedroom, staring at a screen wondering if Oscar and Effie were only pretending everything was okay. I set up a group chat with them on my phone, hoping I might be able to talk to them better that way. But I'd post a message in the morning and spend all day looking at the screen waiting for them to reply. Oscar would eventually say something like he'd been down the park with his friends, and Effie would say she'd been doing stuff with her nan. It was like while I was missing Luke, they were getting on with their lives.

Weren't they missing me, like I was missing them? Weren't they going to sleep with the light on? And when they did fall asleep, weren't they having nightmares about being back down in the mine, and waking up in a pool of sweat because everyone else had gone?

That's what I wanted to ask Oscar and Effie when I saw them. I didn't need to be on a TV show to ask them that ... but as I look up at the stage, I realise it's too late to turn back.

'So,' says Dom Fox, 'that was the story of those incredible days last summer. And I think that, without further ado, we should meet our three heroes.'

The audience claps and cheers. I look across at Oscar. We've been sat here listening for what seems like hours but now there's a woman wearing a pair of headphones with a microphone attached waving at us to go up onto the stage.

'Come on.' She beckons. 'I'll show you the way.'

Oscar stands up and squeezes past his mum and dad's legs.

'Oscar!' I shout. 'What about Effie? She's still not here!'

Oscar looks at the woman and says something I can't hear.

She keeps beckoning.

'Go on, Milo,' says my mum. 'You have to go up on the stage.'

'I know,' I say, standing up. 'But what about Effie? What do you think has happened to her?'

I don't hear Mum's reply, because Dom Fox has now walked to the edge of the stage and is peering down at us. 'It's okay, everyone,' he says. 'Our heroes are on their way.'

Mum and Dad stand up, and I walk past them and join Oscar at the front.

'This is it, Milo.' He beams. 'You get to find out what it's like to be famous like me.'

'But, Oscar,' I say, 'don't you think we should wait?'

But there's no time to wait, because the audience is now cheering and clapping like they've been turned up full blast, and the woman wearing the headset has grabbed me and Oscar by the arms and is leading us to some stairs by the side of the stage.

I follow Oscar up six steps, to where Carly Wyatt meets us.

'Just walk on.' She smiles. 'Dom will look after you.'

I glance back at the exit signs, hoping to see Effie walking through one of them right now. *Where is she?* I ask myself for the twentieth time.

'Ah, here they are,' says Dom. 'Not only did they have us on tenterhooks for those few days, it seems they're doing the same now ... Come on, lads ... and ...' He puts his hand up to the side of his face, like he's checking his earpiece is working. 'Just the boys?' he asks.

276

The woman with the headset nods.

'No worries,' says Dom. 'I'm sure Effie will be along soon enough.' He holds out his arm.

'Oscar Hyatt-Davis from Brighton and Milo Holmes from Bristol, everyone! Our heroes!'

I try to walk but it's like my trainers are stuck in cement.

No, I tell myself. *I can't. I don't want—*

'Come on, Milo.' Oscar pulls my arm. In a second I'm on the stage with bright lights in my face, cameras pointing at me, and beyond them it's dark.

'So, boys,' says Dom. 'Can you tell us how you felt during those days down the mine?'

Oscar starts talking beside me. Something about danger, something about water.

'Was that the scariest time?'

'Yeah.'

'And you, Milo?'

Dom holds a microphone in front of me, but all I can think about are the lights in my face, and the darkness behind, just like the night we came up out of the mine.

'Milo? What was the most worrying time for you?'

I shake my head. Bright lights, darkness. Bright lights, darkness. I'm back in the mine, trapped under a million tonnes of rock, looking up at the light. That's the last time I spoke to him. That's the last time I pictured him in my mind.

I open my mouth.

'My brother,' I say slowly. 'My brother, Luke.'

277

'What's that, Milo? Just a little louder, so the audience and the folks at home can hear. Your brother?'

'Yeah, I left him down there … In … the … mine.'

'Okay.' Dom pulls the microphone away. 'Well, thanks, Milo. We'll just return to Oscar for a moment. Oscar …' Dom's words fade away as I stare out at the lights. They're so bright it feels like they're burning my head. I need to get away from them. I need to get out of here, but I'm scared of the darkness that lies behind.

An arm wraps round my shoulder. Oscar's head is right next to mine.

'It's okay, Milo,' he whispers. 'I know it's the lights. I feel the same.'

I nod. 'Yeah,' I say. 'It's the lights.' I take a breath, then try to take another, but the panic is hitting so bad that I'm suddenly breathing through straws.

'Milo, is everything okay?' Dom, Carly and the woman with the headphones all crowd in on me, so many of them that I don't know who spoke. Then Oscar is shouting.

'He needs to get out of here! I need to get out of here!' Oscar grabs my hand and pulls me along. Too many people, too many voices, too many lights. I cling to Oscar like he's a life raft and I'm never going to let go. Oscar pulls me to the side of the stage, past more people, more lights, metal poles, a red exit sign. We push through a door and burst out into a sunlit car park.

Oscar bends over and puts his hands on his knees. For a moment I think he's going to be sick, but he's just gasping for breath like me.

'It was too soon,' he says. 'The lights, all this. It's too soon.'

I put my hand on his back.

'Yeah,' I gasp. 'Way too soon.'

Oscar puts an arm across my back. 'I thought you were feeling the same,' he says. 'I saw the look on your face.' He stands up and wipes his eyes on his sleeve. 'It was the lights.'

I nod. 'Yes,' I say. 'Like we were being brought back up to the surface again.'

'Only this time one of us is missing.'

'Exactly,' I say. 'But where is she?'

'Right here!'

Me and Oscar spin round.

'Effie!' We both say at the same time.

Effie opens her arms wide.

'Come on, then.' She grins. 'Don't I get a hug?'

Me and Oscar run towards her, then open our arms and wrap them tight around each other.

'I didn't think you were coming,' says Oscar through his tears.

'Me neither,' I say, through mine.

'What are you two like?' says Effie. 'I leave you alone for a few months and you get like this.'

Oscar laughs. 'It's the dust,' he says.

'Yeah, it's the dust,' I agree.

'Of course,' says Effie, holding us tighter. 'It must be the dust.'

I hear a door open, then voices are saying, 'Are you okay?' 'Are they okay?' Then the whir of cameras.

We pull closer and rest our heads together, and it's like for a moment we've closed the rest of the world out. *She's here*, I think to

279

myself. *Oscar too.* All I can hear is the sound of their breathing and the beating of their hearts.

'I'm glad you're here,' I say.

'I'm sorry,' says Effie. 'My nan is lovely, but she wouldn't catch the train, and she also hates driving on the motorway.'

'It's okay,' says Oscar. 'At least we're all here now.'

My heart swells so much it's like it pushes more tears out of my eyes. I knew I was missing Effie, but I suddenly realise how much I've missed Oscar too.

'I think they need space,' says a voice.

'We should give them some time alone,' adds another.

Yes, yes. Please go. Please leave us alone.

I hug Oscar and Effie tighter.

One more camera whir.

Voices fade away.

The click of a door.

Oscar lifts his head. 'I think they've gone,' he says. 'Yeah. They've all gone. At last.'

'What?' says Effie. 'You got tired of being famous already?'

'Yeah,' Oscar says, 'just a bit. Especially when they took a picture of me eating cereal in my pyjamas.'

We all laugh as we let go of each other.

The car park is now empty of reporters. Effie's nan is a few metres away, talking to mine and Oscar's parents.

'So, what happened?' asks Effie. 'What are you doing out here?'

'The lights,' says Oscar. 'It was the lights.'

'You too, Milo?'

'Yeah.' I nod.

Effie smiles. 'I think I'd be the same,' she says. 'How have you both been? I'm sorry I'm rubbish with messaging. It's just ...'

'Just what?' asks Oscar.

'Well,' Effie looks away across the tops of the parked cars, 'I just felt like you two seemed to be doing okay, and ...'

'And?'

'Well, I wasn't. At least not for a long time.'

'Nor me,' says Oscar. 'Milo too.' He nods at me.

'Really?' Effie smiles like she's relieved. 'I thought it was just me ... Does that mean ... No, it sounds daft.'

'It's okay.' Oscar grins. 'We've already said it, haven't we, Milo? We sleep with the light on.'

Effie laughs. 'You've got to tell my nan; she complains I'm using too much electricity.'

I smile.

Effie looks at me, concerned. 'You're quiet, Milo,' she says. 'You okay? I mean, we're all here now.'

'Yeah,' I sigh. I want to speak, but now we're all here, I notice even more that Luke is missing. It was him that did all the talking, it was him that filled in the gaps when my mind went blank. I wish he was here to fill them right now. I want to tell Effie that he's gone, that I'm scared I left him down in the mine in the dark.

'I think Milo has something to tell you,' says Oscar.

I look at him, like, *How do you know?*

Oscar shrugs. 'It's kind of obvious,' he says. 'You've hardly said anything except *Where's Effie?* since we got here.'

'Aw, is that right?' says Effie.

'Pretty much,' I say.

Effie opens her eyes wide at Oscar, telling him to leave us.

'It's okay,' he says. 'I can take a hint.'

'No,' I say, holding on to his arm. 'You can stay.'

'Sure?' he says.

'Yes,' I say, 'I'm sure.'

They both stand and look at me. I've been waiting so long to tell someone, someone who will understand, but the trouble is I need the person I am missing to help me get my thoughts out.

'It's okay,' says Effie. 'Take your time.'

I take a deep breath.

'It's my brother.'

'Luke,' says Effie.

I nod because just hearing his name makes me want to cry.

'He's gone,' I say. 'He doesn't talk to me any more. It's like I left him in the mine.'

For once it's like Oscar can't think of anything to say. He just looks sad for me.

Effie puts her hand on my shoulder.

'Ah, Milo,' she says. 'I'm sorry. Why didn't you message? Or we could have talked.'

'I couldn't,' I said. 'Every time I went to message, it made me upset. And I feel bad, because some days he's not the first thing I think of when I wake up, and not the last person I think about before I go to bed. Sometimes it's you. Sometimes it's even you, Oscar.'

'Thanks for that,' says Oscar. He's trying to be funny but from the look on his and Effie's faces it's like we're all about to cry.

'He's gone,' I say. 'It's like I've forgotten about him.'

Effie wraps her arms around me. 'Milo,' she says, softly. 'You didn't leave him in the mine, and you definitely haven't forgotten about him. You've just moved him from your head to your heart.'

I look at her for a long time and think about what she just said. I've never thought of it that way. I've been missing Luke so much I've not been able to think at all.

I hear a rumbling sound and look up. A plane is crossing the blue sky, leaving smoke trails behind.

Where's it come from?

Where's it going?

Fran San Sico? Hoolahuloo?

I follow the plane as it heads towards the horizon. And for the first time since I came up from the mine it's like I can breathe without my chest aching.

I smile.

Luke, I've not forgotten you, I just moved you from my head to my heart.

I like that.

I like that a lot.

I miss your chicken jokes, and I miss your voice, but now it's like your heart beats with mine.

Oscar puts one arm around my shoulder. Effie does the same. It's like they know what I'm thinking. But suddenly I stop thinking about myself and think about them.

283

'What about you two?' I say. 'How have you been?'

'What? Apart from sleeping with the light on?' Oscar chuckles.

'Yeah,' I say. 'Apart from that.'

'Okay,' says Oscar. 'I mean, my dad turned up to this, so that's a start.'

'I saw,' I say. 'Has he –'

'What about you, Eff?' Oscar cuts across me. 'How have you been?'

'Fine,' says Effie. 'I've got a brilliant nan, so what else do I want?'

Me and Oscar look at her, wondering if anything else has changed.

'What?' she says. 'What else do you want me to say?'

Oscar shrugs.

'Okay,' Effie sighs. 'I thought about writing them – my parents – a letter.'

'You thought?' asks Oscar.

'Yeah,' says Effie. 'I thought … It's a start, Oscar.'

They both laugh. Even when they're spikey with each other, I still love them loads. I reach out and pull them both towards me.

'Friends or enemies?' whispers Oscar.

'Friends, of course,' says Effie. 'Why would you even ask?'

'It's just a thing we do,' says Oscar. 'Isn't it, Milo?'

'Yeah.' I smile. 'It's a thing we do.'

I hug them again, then try to let them go, but I can feel Oscar not wanting me to.

'What's wrong?' I ask.

'Nothing,' he says. 'It's just that something else is missing.'

'Is there?'

'Yep. You know what it is.'

I laugh.

'Okay. You ready?'

'Yep.'

'Promise to laugh, because this was one of his favourites.'

'Go for it,' says Effie.

'Okay. Okay.' I pause for breath because it's the first time I've done it since I came out of the mine. *Here goes*, I tell myself. *Here goes.*

'Why did the chicken cross the road from McDonald's?'

'We don't know,' Oscar and Effie say together. 'Why did the chicken cross the road from McDonald's?'

'Because he saw his brother in *KFC*!'

'That's a good one,' says Oscar.

Yeah, I think to myself, *that's a good one.*

And I knew Luke would think it was too.

READ MORE BOOKS FROM THE
AWARD-WINNING STEWART FOSTER!

TURN THE PAGE TO READ THE FIRST
CHAPTER OF THE PHENOMENAL

CAN YOU FEEL THE NOISE?

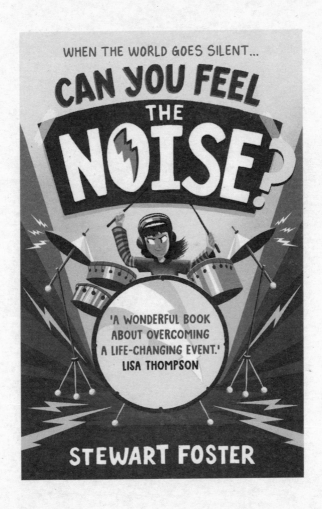

CHAPTER 1

THE NOISE

It started as a distant hum. A low drilling noise, like roadworks had begun on my street one Sunday morning. It was so real I kept checking out of my bedroom window for white vans and workers digging in reflective clothing. But there was no one there, except for a boy from the house four doors down, kicking his football against a wall.

The hum was still there in the afternoon.

'Perhaps it's the fridge,' my mum suggested. 'It's on its way out.'

'Or maybe it's the electricity pylon down the road,' said my dad.

'No,' I said. 'The fridge is more of a drone, and the pylon is a buzz – this is as irritating as both but is neither.'

They shrugged because they couldn't hear a noise anything like the one I was describing, but they could tell how annoyed I was, because Dad was still trying to help identify what it was during tea.

'Are you sure it's not the pylon?' he said. 'Only, you know I'm fairly sure it causes my psoriasis.'

'Dad,' I snapped, and put my knife and fork down. 'It's not the pylon. You blame everything on it – your psoriasis, your bald patch, the grass not growing.'

'Only trying to help, Soph,' he said, like I'd upset him.

'I know,' I said. 'I'm sorry – it's just the noise has been there all day, like a million midges, midging away at my brain.'

'Midging?' Mum chuckled.

'Well,' I said, 'whatever it is that midges do.'

We all laughed, then Mum put her hand on mine.

'Perhaps it's wax, Soph,' she said gently. 'I'll put some olive oil in your ears before you go to bed.'

That night I went to bed, ears so greasy I felt like my head was slipping off the pillow. But the noise was still there. For a while, I thought it was my stepbrother, Liam, outside with his friends revving their motorbikes, even though I was sure I'd heard him come in at eleven. I was doubly sure it was him when I sniffed the smell of burnt toast wafting under my door.

But that didn't stop me getting up and checking three more times during the night. My alarm clock said 2.05 a.m. the next time I got up.

2.26 a.m. the next.

3.09 a.m. the time after that.

It had to be something, somewhere – a truck, or a bus idling – but each time I looked, all I saw was the neighbourhood cats stalking each other under the village street lights.

That day in May was the first time I had the noise, but it wasn't the first problem I'd had with my ears.

I'd noticed it first in the final term at my primary school, six months ago, whenever Mrs Santo turned her back and wrote a sum on the whiteboard. As she spoke, all I could hear was the mumble of her voice, just loud enough that I could make out how many syllables she was saying. Most times I could see what she'd written, and would be able to answer, but if she asked another question after that, I wouldn't be able to work out what she'd said. I'd sit still, feeling dumb, while other kids in the class were waving their hands in the air.

The first person I told was Mum, and it turned out she wasn't surprised. She'd noticed how every day it felt like she was having to shout louder up the stairs to tell me when tea was ready. She'd thought that I'd been ignoring her, or maybe I had been too immersed in playing my songs on my guitar.

She took me to see a hearing consultant, Dr Cowans. He gave me a test and said my hearing wasn't as good as it could be, and that we should monitor it for a while. A month later, I didn't need another test to know my hearing was getting worse. I could still hear, but I was now sometimes missing questions, even when Mrs Santo was facing the class, and I'd have to ask my friend Mia what she'd said. And over the summer holidays, Mum and Dad had noticed that I'd started turning the TV up louder.

I began to notice it more when I started at Cromwell High. It might have been because the classes were bigger and the students noisier, but I had to sit near the front to hear the teachers. Luckily at my last appointment with Dr Cowans a few months ago, he said my hearing seemed to have stabilized; while it wasn't getting better, it didn't seem to be getting any worse. Which made me feel great – it finally felt like things were starting to look up.

But the morning the noise started, it didn't feel like things were looking up; it felt like they were getting worse.

It was still with me when I got on the bus to school with Mia the next morning. My noise was irritating me so much that I didn't want to talk about it; I thought Mia might think it was weird. Besides, she seemed more preoccupied with how I smelt.

'What is it?' she said, sniffing the air as she looked at me.

'Maybe it's my deodorant,' I said.

'No.' Mia leaned close. 'It's not that.'

'Maybe Mum's changed our fabric conditioner.' I held out my arm for her to smell.

'No.' She screwed up her face.

'What is it, then?' I asked. 'Because you're making me feel gross.'

Mia didn't answer, and we hardly talked as the bus drove out of our village. I just stared out of the window because I'd gone to bed with the noise, woken up with the noise, eaten breakfast with the noise, and now it was still there, whining away above the rumble of the bus wheels. I closed my eyes, took deep breaths to try to calm down, but it was still there like an alarm clock, ringing in my head. I just wished I could reach up with my hand, slam the button and turn it off.

Mia didn't say much in registration either, but then sometimes we're like that. Being friends for five years, we don't have to talk to know how the other is feeling. She knew I was irritable in the same way I knew she was upset when Lotto, her dog, died. We just don't have to spend all day reminding each other what's on our minds. She's in the band with me. In fact, we were the ones who started it in the second week after winter break.

We were sat together at lunch, playing our guitars, when two boys from our year came and joined us – Ty and Rocco. They often came to the music room, but we'd never spoken to them before. They said they'd heard us playing songs that they liked, like 'Fade Away' and 'Dying Sun', and Ty showed us his rucksack where he'd painted the band name BURNOUT in big yellow letters on to the back of it.

That's the moment I knew we'd get along, and we decided to form a band, with Ty on keyboard and Rocco as our lead singer. We played for fun more than anything else and hadn't even come up with a name when our music teacher, Mrs Hopkirk, said we should enter the Battle of the Bands competition to find the best school band in our area. We've already got through the first round with HiFi Dad from Year Nine and a group of sixth-formers called the Longshots, and we're all playing in the semi-finals in three weeks' time. The final is at Rock City, the biggest music venue in town, two weeks after that. We spend most of our lunchtimes practising in the music room, and today was like any other. Except this time, I had my noise, and all anyone could talk about was the weird smell.

'Chips!' Rocco said. 'That's what it is! You smell of chips.'

'What?' I sniffed my arms again.

'Chips!' He seemed almost happy about it. 'But don't worry, sometimes I know I stink of my dad's homemade beer. It's not your clothes; it's your hair.'

'No, it's not,' I said. 'Is it?' I pulled a band out of my hair. 'Oh no, it is,' I said, lifting my hair up to my nose. 'It's everywhere.'

'What is?' asked Mia.

'Olive oil,' I said.

'Olive oil?' they all said at the same time.

'Yeah,' I said. 'I've got this noise in my head. A high-pitched whine. My mum thought it might be trapped wax, so she put olive oil in my ear to loosen it.'

'Gross,' said Rocco, scrunching up his nose.

'Thanks, Rocco,' I said. 'I know it makes it look like I haven't washed it for week.'

'True.'

'You're not supposed to agree with me,' I said irritably.

'Just saying.' Rocco smirked.

I turned to Ty, who had cranked his amp up so loud it hummed. 'And can you at least keep that down until we're ready to play?'

'Haven't touched it,' said Ty.

'You have,' I snapped at him like I had at Dad the night before. 'I can hear it.'

'Soph, it's not.' Ty lifted up his keyboard lead. 'It's not even plugged in.'

'Then what is it? That hum.'

The band looked at each other.

'Can't you hear it?' I said, panicking. 'Please tell me you can hear it.'

'There's no noise, Soph,' said Mia. 'You know we've not turned the amps up loud since your doctor said not to.'

I suddenly felt hot and like I was trapped in a box. The noise was in my head, and it had followed me from home to school. But it was changing: one minute it was a rumbling truck engine, the next it was like I was being followed by a screeching alien. Now it was like a thousand bees stuck in a jar. At first it was annoying, but now I'd started to freak out.

I put my guitar down beside me and sat on a desk. I wanted to leave, but we'd just got through the first round of Battle of the Bands and needed to practise as much as we could. We had the semi-finals coming up, then if we got through, the finals were at Rock City, in the centre of town.

Rocco came over to me like he could tell I was worried.

'It's okay, Soph,' he said. 'Maybe just sit here quietly and write some lyrics instead.' Then he went off, bouncing around while pretending he was singing into a microphone. He could be an idiot sometimes, but he could almost always make me smile. I couldn't smile then, though, and I definitely couldn't think of any lyrics, not with the noise *buzz*, *buzz*, *buzzing* in my head.

When I got home from school, I went straight to my room. Mum came in and asked if I was okay. I told her the noise was still there. She told me she'd call Dr Cowans in the morning to make an appointment. I knew I had to go. I'd been six times in the last year, but still I hated having the cold metal probe in my ear, like a tiny telescope with a light shining through. And I hated having my ears tested, which might have been why Mum let me eat my tea in my bedroom ... or maybe she knew I didn't want to hear Dad going on about the pylons.

That evening, I tried to do my history homework, but the harder

I concentrated, the worse the noise got. I turned on the TV to try to cover it, but it was still there, like a pack of hyenas, screaming in the middle of my head. I tried playing music, I tried putting my hands over my ears, I tried wrapping my head in my pillow, but there was no escape.

After two hours, my phone buzzed beside me.

A message from Rocco.

Rocco: Hey, Soph are you okay?
Still got the 🐝?

Sophie: Yes. Still there.

Rocco: Hope it goes. I got a song for next round of Battle of the Bands.

I smiled even though my noise had made me so tired.

Sophie: How does it go? It better not be about a 🐝

Rocco: It's not ☺ Hang on . . .

I looked at my phone, imagined Rocco in his garage recording his song idea. He couldn't play drums, but when we were together, he'd play me simple beats he'd find on the internet and then we'd sit side by side and he'd sing the tune and I'd add the melody and the lyrics.

My screen lit up as a file from Rocco arrived.

I opened it up.

A simple drumbeat played, then Rocco began to sing '*la-la-la*' over the top of it. I smiled. Rocco had a good voice, but it was weird without lyrics.

Rocco: What do you think?

Sophie: It's a good tune.

Rocco: Cool. We could work on it tomorrow?

Sophie: Could do, but I might have to go to hospital as Mum's calling them in the morning.

Rocco: About the 🐝?
Just swat it 🏸

Sophie: I'll try.

Rocco: Maybe that's what we should call the band. The Bees 😊 Or the Swats 😊

My phone kept vibrating as Rocco sent more names, but my noise was wearing me out.

I put the phone down on my bedside table and switched off the light. For a moment I thought about Battle of the Bands, imagining us all at Rock City, with me and Mia playing guitars and Ty standing behind the keyboard, while Rocco jumped around onstage like Tigger from *Winnie the Pooh*. I smiled, but that soon disappeared as the noise came back again – the hyenas had gone, but the bees were back. Like they were stuck in the corner of a window trying to get out.

It didn't matter which way I tried to sleep – it was always there. So bad, I felt like swatting it with one of my music books, just like Rocco had said. The next minute it didn't sound like a bee at all. It was like I was watching a monster in a scary film, creeping and crawling. If it *had* been a film, I would've jumped up and turned it off before it got to the scary bit, but this noise didn't have a switch – it was in the middle of my head.